DARK WHISPERS
A Novel of the Abbadon Inn

WELCOME TO THE ABBADON INN.

It's on a quiet street in the charming Victorian town of Cape May, New Jersey. Built in the late 1850s as a rooming house by the enigmatic Nicholas Abbadon, the Inn has been used over the years as a brothel, a restaurant, a speakeasy . . . and more.

SETTLE IN.

It has withstood war, fire, and flood. It has survived the suspicions about the guests who died there and owners who disappeared, the rumors about what went on behind the closed doors of the third floor, and the whispers about Abbadon and his mysterious female companion.

Abandoned and vacant for years, it's ready for renovation. But as a new generation is about to discover, the Abbadon Inn has never really been empty at all . . .

ENJOY YOUR STAY.

DARK WHISPERS

A Novel of the Abbadon Inn

Chris Blaine

BERKLEY BOOKS, NEW YORK

THE BERKLEY PUBLISHING GROUP
Published by the Penguin Group
Penguin Group (USA) Inc.
375 Hudson Street, New York, New York 10014, USA
Penguin Group (Canada), 90 Eglinton Avenue East, Suite 700, Toronto, Ontario M4P 2Y3, Canada
(a division of Pearson Penguin Canada Inc.)
Penguin Books Ltd., 80 Strand, London WC2R 0RL, England
Penguin Group Ireland, 25 St. Stephen's Green, Dublin 2, Ireland (a division of Penguin Books Ltd.)
Penguin Group (Australia), 250 Camberwell Road, Camberwell, Victoria 3124, Australia
(a division of Pearson Australia Group Pty. Ltd.)
Penguin Books India Pvt. Ltd., 11 Community Centre, Panchsheel Park, New Delhi—110 017, India
Penguin Group (NZ), Cnr. Airborne and Rosedale Roads, Albany, Auckland 1310, New Zealand
(a division of Pearson New Zealand Ltd.)
Penguin Books (South Africa) (Pty.) Ltd., 24 Sturdee Avenue, Rosebank, Johannesburg 2196,
South Africa

Penguin Books Ltd., Registered Offices: 80 Strand, London WC2R 0RL, England

DARK WHISPERS

A Berkley Book/published by arrangement with the author

PRINTING HISTORY
Berkley mass-market edition/October 2005

Copyright © 2005 The Berkley Publishing Group.
Cover art by Steven Ferlauto.
Interior art by Cortney Skinner.
Interior text design by Kristin del Rosario.

ISBN: 0-425-20629-7

BERKLEY® BOOKS
Berkley Books are published by The Berkley Publishing Group,
a division of Penguin Group (USA) Inc.,
375 Hudson Street, New York, New York 10014.
The name BERKLEY and the BERKLEY design are trademarks belonging to Penguin Group (USA) Inc.

PRINTED IN THE UNITED STATES OF AMERICA

10 9 8 7 6 5 4 3 2 1

This one's for Barbara—my roommate at the haunted hotel.

Thanks also go to Team Abbadon—Ginjer, Beth, Cort, Matt, and most especially Craig (he knows why). And to Team Boston—Mary, Victoria, Rich, and Jeff. And last, but far from least, to the nice folks at the Queen's Hotel in Cape May, who not only answered my questions but showed me their basement!

The Window where we saw the face

Abbadon Inn 1948

Nicholas Abbadon

C.G. MITCHELL, Photographer
CAPE MAY, NEW JERSEY

The Abbadon Inn, first opened in 1856, welcomes the weary traveller with comfortable lodging, fine meals, and special entertainments not found in any other establishment in Cape May.

CAPE MAY
JAN 11
8 AM

POST CARD

27855

Aug. 10 1933
Hello Harry—
Mildred and I booked a room here for the week. Nicholas Abbadon, while a gracious host, has an odd presence. Last night Mildred awoke, screaming that Mr. Abbadon was watching her. We will spend the remaining vacation elsewhere.
Your brother, J

The Abbadon Inn
Cape May, New Jersey
CLOSE COVER BEFORE STRIKING

ABBADON INN
Cape May, N.J.

PROLOGUE

1962

You couldn't hear the wind, way down here, couldn't feel the rain. It didn't matter.

There was still no way out.

Cooney almost laughed at the thought. He had come here, to Cape May on the Jersey Shore, as part of his way back in. That had been most of a year ago. The war in Korea was long done. He had re-upped, with the foolish idea that he could be a peacetime soldier. The Army had still managed to give him an honorable discharge four years later, despite that little trouble toward the end. He had even gone to college for a while on the G.I. Bill. Everything was aces. Until he ended up in a cellar waiting for who knew what.

Back in Korea, Cooney had made a hell of a soldier. They could send him anywhere, tell him to do anything, and he would get the job done.

He discovered early on that he liked it better if the job involved pain. At first, he thought he liked to hurt the enemy. Later, he realized he just really liked to hurt, period. Mostly, he liked to kill. No. It was more like he liked to watch people die.

None of that changed when he had gotten back stateside. Until Cooney got careless. The Army couldn't prove just who had done what to the pimp and those three hookers. Not that they ever found most of the pimp. The guy got what he deserved trying to run a scam on returning servicemen. Cooney had tried to get rid of the bodies in the usual way, but there were too many at one time. And one of the hookers had been underage.

The Army knew Cooney was involved in the whole bloody mess somehow. Whatever he had done was "a potential stain on the Armed Services." Thanks to his war record, they kept Cooney's profile clean as they showed him the door.

He'd decided to improve himself then, going to Michigan State on the G.I. Bill. He dabbled in psychology, English literature, even chemistry during the couple of years he had managed to kick around there. If only he had been able to ignore those smug fraternity guys. But there were some things Cooney could never ignore. The car wreck looked enough like an accident—it was obvious that all four young men had been drinking—in those days, as long as they could close the books, the locals didn't look all that closely. Cooney still knew it was time to move on.

But what do you do when you're back on the streets and your only real talent is holding a gun? America was the land of opportunity, the place to get married and have a couple kids while you worked your way up in the company. Cooney didn't even want to walk through the company doors.

He ran through two or three dead-end jobs, even flirted with the idea of taking a police exam. But the jobs always ended in arguments or worse. The third one ended in assault charges. That killed any thought of the police exam. The police didn't like guys who got into fights before they were in a cop's uniform.

Then things got interesting. The guy Cooney put in the hospital owed money to other guys—connected guys who took notice of Cooney's abilities. They took him aside, told Cooney about the newly crippled guy's debt. The cripple was never going to pay that debt now. Cooney owed them.

Cooney started, shaking his head free of memories. He'd heard a noise from somewhere upstairs. It was hard to tell in this old inn. Sometimes you could hear somebody slam a door two floors away, the clank of pots and pans in the kitchen when you were out in the street, or a woman's laughter from behind a closed window across the street. The building itself would make noises, too, as if the rotting wood was so old it could no longer keep still. Stairs seemed to creak by themselves, windows rattled on the quietest of days, and on truly stormy nights, the whole inn seemed to sigh along with the wind.

They had their share of storms here in Cape May, but Cooney had never experienced a storm like this one. The radio—he hadn't brought down the radio!—but he had heard on the radio that the storm was flooding out whole parts of the shore, even dragging entire buildings out to sea.

It was still dry here in the cellar. The whole damn town could wash away, and this inn would stay high and dry. If there was one thing that Cooney had found out in his months living in this place, it was that the Abbadon had its own rules.

Cooney sat quietly, barely breathing. He just had to figure out which noises were real, and which ones would leave him dead.

He heard it again—*clump, clump, clump*—it sounded now like someone in heavy boots crossing the worn floor of the kitchen above. They really were coming for him now. It would end here, after all these weeks. They would have to show themselves at last.

Cooney waited in silence. He had picked the storeroom beneath the kitchen as the best place to defend himself. He had thought about running, but dismissed the idea almost as soon as it had come. He couldn't live the rest of his life looking over his shoulder. If a bullet was coming, he wanted to face it now.

The footsteps stopped almost directly overhead. Whoever was upstairs seemed to be waiting, too. Cooney could hear nothing but his breathing and the deep wet booming of his heart. His piece shone dimly beneath the twenty-five-watt bulbs strung along the ceiling down here. He had always felt better with a gun in his hand. But the Smith & Wesson was cold beneath his fingers.

It was always freezing in the cellar, no matter what season it was above, no matter how much that furnace in the corner roared. Cooney was sweating anyway. He had to wipe the perspiration from his eyes. His shirt stuck to his back.

They had waited for the storm to come for him. Smart. Who would notice one more missing body when the ocean was claiming half the town?

He'd be better once they showed. He had brought an old chair down with him to put on the dirt floor, then jammed himself into a corner of the room that had a clear shot at both doors—the ways they'd have to come for him. He'd go on automatic—like he always did. The others would be dead before they could even think. Cooney always got every one.

Every one. He glanced up at the ceiling beams. Why weren't they moving up there?

He was out of place. He wasn't the one holding the cards. Even with the big boys calling the shots, the Family figured out Cooney's limits. Now it was like there were no limits at all.

It was funny, thinking about the last time he felt this much at odds with his life. He remembered how much he had resisted—at first—when the Family tried to haul him in.

They were big guys in slick Italian suits that didn't quite hide the bulge of their guns. They smiled when they said Cooney owed them. They were used to intimidating people. Cooney had only smiled back. Even then, he realized the way they talked sounded a little bit like he was coming home.

The suits had taken his grin in stride, until one of the guys leaned on Cooney a little too hard. They wanted the money now, did they? Cooney had held back and only broke the suit's arm. He had half-expected them to try to kill him after that. But the suits respected talent. They saw how quick he was, how he broke bones with no wasted effort. They saw the way he smiled when he heard the *snap*.

And they knew they could always kill him later. So they started asking questions.

They figured out Cooney could break bones. How did he feel about murder? In a matter of months, Cooney had proved he could do just about anything they asked. On the Jersey Shore, they paid well for that kind of work. And Cooney was so good at it, they let him kill people just about any way he wanted.

The war was over. America was going places. Times were good for everybody, and everybody wanted their piece of the pie, including the mob. If you didn't play ball, you got to see Cooney. He could get in and out of some place before they even knew he was there. Guys used to call him "the ghost."

The ghost. It was a joke to the boys, seeing as how the Abbadon Inn looked a little like something out of one of those Abbott and Costello comedies full of ghosts and monsters. It was a joke to everybody but their boss. The more he heard about the ghosts, the more the big man thought the spirits could explain everything that had gone wrong. Toward the end there, Tito was jumping at his own shadow.

It was amazing how quickly everything fell apart. But when Cooney had first been recruited he had thought he had it made. As the months and years went by, it had all been good as he worked his way up in the organization, until he'd gotten a promotion to a whole other level. He'd risen about as high as you could go in the organization, if you weren't born into it. These last few months he had had to spend a lot of his time protecting Tito and the big boys—the top guys in the Family. It wasn't anywhere near as interesting as the other part of his job, but it paid so well that Cooney made sure he was good at it. And he had been good, too, up until now. Until the wrong people had started to die.

Uncle Freddy was the first, found with a knife in his chest in the kitchen right above where Cooney waited. Then it was Sal the Barber, at four A.M., strangled outside the toolshed, right behind the inn's kitchen.

Rumors flew among the New Jersey families. The Feds were on to them. A mob from New York or Philly (reports varied) was looking to expand. Some crazed vigilante group was trying to clean up the resort town.

Vinnie Fishhooks was next. They found him in a room on the top floor, without a mark on him, his face frozen, eyes and mouth wide, like he was in the middle of a scream.

That's when Cooney saw the connection.

It was the Abbadon Inn.

All the guys had died in or around the old inn. When Gino was found in the cellar, it only confirmed his suspicions. And then with what happened to Sheila—

Some locals had a vendetta. Cooney thought the boys should have expected something of the sort. After all, the Family hadn't been shy about announcing their plans.

He remembered when they first took a look around their property, right after he had been promoted to protection; how Tito had laughed about the place. The Family had taken the ramshackle structure in payment for a bad debt, after which the former owner had killed himself. Or that's what the cops had said.

The inn was a big, rambling structure, an old Victorian place. It could be charming, Sheila had said, if you put some money into it. Yeah, Tito had replied. Too much money. Tito said he'd tear it down and use the lot for something new, some part of a new, luxury hotel Tito was planning to put right on the boardwalk. Tito liked to think ahead. Someday, his guys were going to bring gambling right to the Jersey Shore.

No one would question Tito. Nobody could stand up to the Family. They had money. They had politicians in their pockets. When all else failed, they had guns.

But it looked like somebody was standing up to them after all.

People around Tito were dying, no two deaths alike. So maybe there were wacko vigilantes after all. It made a certain crazy sense. You couldn't kill every member of the mob. But maybe you could scare them away.

Cooney had to admit, the scare stuff was certainly working on those around him. The day before yesterday, after Sheila's body was found, Tito suddenly had to take "a business trip" somewhere out of state, and soon as he was gone, his lieutenants had split to check out this and that in other parts of Jersey. They'd left the inn to Cooney and two other guys.

Hey, they called him the ghost. How could you kill a ghost?

But up until now, it hadn't all been bad. Cape May had given him Lucy, sweet Lucy, a woman who reminded him of what his life had been before Korea, someone he might really love, and let him leave this world behind. Why couldn't he have gone away with Lucy? Why couldn't the world be a different place?

Well, it wasn't, and he was left here, all alone. Cooney hadn't seen the other guys for hours. But he had heard somebody scream.

He had thought the scream had come from somewhere in the basement and had come down to investigate, but he'd seen no sign of the other two. Once he'd gotten down here, he'd taken a look at the solid stone walls and the couple of small, dirty windows, the single stairway coming down from the hotel, the single door leading out. If the vigilantes were coming for him, he decided this was as good a place as any to make a stand.

Still no noise. Cooney wondered if he should move around. His palms were damp despite the cold. He shifted his gun from hand to hand, wiping his palms on his two-hundred-dollar pants. According to Sheila, the original owners had used these rooms for storage before the days of electricity. There were still some old gaslight fixtures down here. Just as well he was alone, he guessed. If anyone saw him now, Cooney would lose his rep as a stone-cold killer.

The noises started up again, a clatter, this time, like a dozen guys coming down the stairs from the second floor.

Whoever was coming wasn't being quiet about it.

Did they know he was waiting? Maybe it was one of the other guys. Maybe Cooney wasn't the last man standing after all.

He crouched behind a barrel, his gun raised to take out the first person to show himself at the door.

Again, they stopped making noises. This was driving him crazy. He had to know.

"Charlie?" he called. "Walt?"

No answer, of course.

Cooney was finding it hard to breathe.

He blinked. The light was all wrong.

He was surrounded by water. The basement was gone. He saw sunlight, close above, but he couldn't reach the surface. Hands were holding him down. He struggled, but his fingers were small and old. He looked at the hands holding him down and recognized a big gold ring. It was his ring.

The hands that were killing him were his own.

He flashed back to the Korean woman he had killed, just weeks before the end of the war. It was too bad she had shown him her box of valuables.

Now it felt like his own hands were around Cooney's throat.

They said your life flashed before you, just before you died. Cooney never thought it would be like this.

The water was gone. He felt an instant of searing pain as the bullet burrowed into his chest. He saw his own face again, Cooney smiling, Cooney laughing, as he was pushed off a Trenton tenement to die on the street below. And on and on. How many had Cooney killed? How many times did he need to die?

Whatever was happening, Cooney wouldn't let it take him. He was stronger than this. He could swallow the fear and piss away the pain.

He blinked again. He was back in the cellar. He wouldn't let them get to him. Lucy, he thought. He'd remember the good times with Lucy. She was always his savior when things went bad.

Cooney shook his head. It had always been better when Lucy was with him. Korea, the mob, the killings, he didn't need to think about any of it if he could only see Lucy's smile.

He wouldn't think about the other part, what happened after.

But he wasn't alone. He could hear them now, in the shadows. The gun was still in his hand.

It was all about the Abbadon Inn. And everyone here was meant to die.

The back door flew open with a sound like a gunshot. Rain and snow flew into the cellar, water washed down the steps. The ocean was rushing to claim the Abbadon.

He turned to the stairs that led back into the hotel. The water was above his shoes, swirling about his ankles, threatening to rise to his knees. If he didn't get out of here, he would drown. He looked up the stairs and stopped. A single figure was walking down the steps toward him, the last person he had ever expected to see. Even in the dim light of the cellar, he could see her quite clearly; the slim figure, the long legs, the pale oval face framed by long, chestnut hair. She was wearing the same dress she had worn the last night they had been together—that terrible, terrible night.

And now, despite all that had happened, she had come back to him.

She smiled and replied to his unasked question. "How could I stay away?"

Cooney pushed himself forward through the rising

water, determined to make the stairs before the flood overwhelmed him. One word tore from his throat, the only word that mattered.

Her name.

"Lucy!" he cried. He could almost reach the stairway's railing, but the water was above his waist, swirling about him, wanting to suck him down below the surface, and to keep him there forever.

ONE

1986

"What say we get out of the rain?" John Dalton said to his wife as they both climbed onto the protective cover of the porch—their porch—the porch of the just-purchased and soon-to-be-reopened Abbadon Inn. It was a grand Victorian in the midst of a row of the same, in the most desirable part of town, two blocks from the beach. And it was all theirs.

The front door stuck when he tried it the first time. John Dalton laughed. There was no way he was going to be kept out of this place. Right now, he was ready to beat anything. He pushed the keys the realtor had given him back into the lock, wriggled them back and forth, heard the mechanism open and close. Nothing wrong with the lock. He rattled the knob. The door still wouldn't give. He glanced back at his wife, Karen, who stood just behind him on the porch—their porch. "Looks like this place is already putting us to work."

She laughed. "I guess we'd better get used to it."

He twisted the knob as he put his shoulder to the door. The door popped open with a groan.

"Doesn't sound very welcoming," Karen said, as she walked in behind him.

"Now that we own this place, I guess it no longer has to be on its best behavior," he replied. They had been in and out of this old building more than a dozen times in the last month as they finalized their purchase. But it was only this morning that they had signed on the bottom line; only this morning the realtor had handed them their keys. And it was a truly dreary February morning—a day when the weather couldn't decide between snow and freezing rain, so different from the bright January days when they had toured the property before. The place had looked so promising, the last great Victorian in a line of half a dozen of the big houses, lacking only a coat of paint to make it as bright as its neighbors.

Nothing was particularly bright on a day like this. The old wood would swell up in this kind of weather. And the door stick. He pushed the door shut behind them. This time it closed just fine.

"Just one more thing to add to the list."

"The never-ending list," his wife replied as she stepped up beside him. But when he looked her way, he saw that she was smiling, too.

"Hey, we're going to show this old inn who's boss." He glanced around the small lobby in front of him. Without the bustle of the real estate agent, the inspectors, the contractors—a dozen or more people who had walked these halls in the past few weeks—the place seemed unusually quiet.

A thin coating of dust had settled everywhere, turning the walls and floor to shades of gray. That seemed new since their last walk-through, less than a week before. Apparently, they had a lot of old dirt to clean up in this place. He flipped a switch. At least the lights were working. But the outside cold had crept into the inside air. He could even see his breath here in the lobby.

"We've got to get the furnace going." It should have been on low, even now, to keep the pipes from freezing—they had made an agreement with the agent.

He waved for his wife to follow. "Let's see what we've gotten ourselves into."

John walked the length of the place, past the lobby and the stairs leading to the second floor, then through a short hall that opened into the dining room and finally back into the kitchen. There had been some sort of accident in here, a year or more back. A small fire, too, but no damage that wasn't easily fixed. They would get carpenters in to pull up the damaged flooring and get the place updated in a couple other areas. John hoped they could be done with the first floor in a matter of days.

He looked around at the porcelain sinks, the large oven, the walk-in refrigerator, a row of hanging iron skillets that had been left behind. A lot of the stuff in here couldn't be more than a few years old.

Apparently, the last owner had died. The real estate agent didn't seem to know much more than that. She said the place was a steal, twenty percent lower than anything else on the market. The original asking price had still been a bit beyond their means, even with his mother's bequest, but John and Karen had fallen in love with the place. What did they have to lose? So they had made an even lower offer—one they could still just barely afford. They were amazed when the former owner's family had accepted.

John wondered why the previous owners had let this beautiful old structure—a great, rambling Victorian, just blocks from the ocean—go so cheaply. The other day, the inspector had said something about the old owners having family problems. In a place like Cape May, apparently everybody knew everybody else's business. The inspector hadn't said much else about the former owners, but John could imagine. He knew all about family problems. When he'd talked to Karen about it later, she had said not to worry about other people's dirty laundry. The only thing that concerned them now was their own good fortune.

John supposed he might have bad feelings about a place, too, if somebody he knew had died here. But that was someone else's history. They were going to turn this place around and make it like it was brand new— a fresh start both for the Victorian Abbadon Inn and what they did with the rest of their lives.

Karen walked into the kitchen. "And just how long is it going to take to make this place livable?"

"Hey, it's perfectly livable now. If you're a polar bear. Or maybe a penguin."

From his wife's less-than-happy expression, it was clear that she didn't exactly appreciate his keen observations. But they weren't going to get anything done standing around in the cold.

"I'll get the furnace going. The inspector said when it's running on low, sometimes a draft can knock it out."

Karen hugged her arms close to her coat. "Well, if it's one thing this place has, it's drafts."

He hoped that was all there was to it. The last owners had installed a special switch for just this problem. If there was nothing wrong with the oil flow to the furnace, one touch of a button would send a spark to get the whole thing up and running.

He opened the door to the basement and hit the red RESTART button at the top of the stairs. He heard the furnace whoosh back to life.

He turned back to his wife. "Mission accomplished!"

Karen grinned at John. "Now that's my home handyman."

He grinned back at her. If this was going to be the worst of their problems, it might be smooth sailing after all.

"Somebody left us some mail. It was on the table in the hall." She held out a stack of envelopes and papers held together with a rubber band. "Looks like it's mostly junk. Flyers. A free copy of the local paper."

As she passed the pile of mail to John, a single envelope fluttered to the floor. She bent down to pick it up.

"What's that?" he asked.

She glanced more closely at the pinched script on the envelope's front, then held it out to him. "It's a letter. From your sister."

Every happy thought left his head, as though it had been washed away by a gust of the freezing rain.

"It's starting already, then," he said as he took the letter.

"John?"

Her husband, so full of energy only a moment before, now stood frozen in the middle of the kitchen, staring at a piece of paper in his hands.

Karen had hoped for better than this.

This whole Abbadon Inn thing had seemed almost too good to be true from the first. Bought with the money from John's mother's will, everything had fallen into place in a matter of weeks. It felt as though it was meant to be. It felt like the beginning of a whole new life.

"It's only a letter," she insisted. "You haven't even opened it!" Her husband didn't react at all.

Maybe, Karen thought, it had all happened a little too quickly. She could see the stress in John's face. Even though they had moved someplace new, they were still using far too much energy to run away from their old lives. Apparently, those problems were going to follow them no matter how far they ran.

Well, they had the inn now, and hundreds of plans for what to do with it. They had rented a motel room with a kitchenette in town on a weekly basis for a ridiculously small amount of money; maybe one-tenth of what they would pay for any place in town during the high season. It would give them a chance to fix a few things before they moved in.

Their remaining money was a little tight—they wouldn't be able to do everything they wanted right away. But they could do some things. Maybe if they could make some tiny bits of progress—clean the place, make some minor repairs, add a new coat of paint—they could feel like this was truly their new home.

John sighed. "Well, I guess I have to open it sometime."

Karen rubbed her husband's shoulder. They had both had things in Manhattan that they wanted to leave behind. John had wanted to put some distance between him and his father, but apparently the entire length of New Jersey wasn't far enough. The letter had found them as soon as they had walked into the hotel. Karen supposed she should have expected it. John's family had never let him do anything on his own, except, in his father's words, be "a damn failure" time after time. Why should this be any different?

"Read it to me," she said.

He ripped open the envelope and pulled out a single sheet of stationery inside. He scanned the page, noting "It's short and sweet." He began to read.

" 'Dear John and Karen,

" 'So glad to hear you've finally bought a place of your own. I've canceled all my appointments to give you a hand and help you get settled. Ralph and I will be driving down on Friday. Expect us mid-afternoon.

" 'I'm so happy for you. I'm sure we can find all sorts of ways to help. This is the kind of thing families need to do together.

" 'Love,

" 'Angela.' "

John looked up at Karen, trying to force his face into a

grin. Karen felt the anger welling inside her. The letter seemed so innocuous. One had to know John's family to see what was really going on behind it. John couldn't do anything without them. Their idea of help was to push him aside and take control. The youngest brother's continued failure was an ironclad part of the family structure.

She shook her head. "Tomorrow? That's fast even for them."

"As usual." John put the letter down on the counter, as if he no longer wanted to touch it. "They give us no way out."

Her husband sounded defeated.

"How did they find out about the sale so quickly?" she asked.

"Well, real estate sales are a matter of public record."

Karen laughed. Even she could hear the bitterness in her voice. "We only signed the papers yesterday! This letter was written days ago."

John shrugged. "Maybe my father has somebody following us. Maybe they have every petty official in New Jersey on their payroll. With the Dalton empire, anything is possible."

She had trouble accepting that they were just going to take whatever the family dished out. The Daltons were intruding before John and Karen even had a chance to get started.

"Maybe we never opened that letter," she suggested. "Maybe we could be out of town for a day or two."

John shook his head. "We'd just be delaying things. We have to find some way of dealing with whatever they throw at us. I'm the one who's had to live with them for over thirty years. There's lots of ways they can still screw things up. So we'll be polite—but no more than polite. We're going to be too busy to say much more than hello. It's good the place isn't ready to take in any guests, isn't it?"

As John talked, she could hear the strength push back into his tone. Maybe they would be able to stand up to them after all.

It was the all-too-simple, all-too-complex life of the Daltons. His father's money spoke to a lot of people. She had come to realize in three years of marriage that his family was nothing but negative. And they had a way of dripping their bile into everything John did.

John dropped the letter on the counter and walked around the kitchen, opening and closing the empty cabinets that rose above the counter on either side. Karen found herself staring out the window at the rain.

She had needed to get away from New York, too. As John had grown more unhappy over these last three years, more ground-down under the family heel, she had started looking for escape as well. She had tried to get away in all the wrong ways, looked for love in all the wrong places, had the world's worst and most miserable affair. It had been over almost before it began. And it made Karen realize one thing. All she really wanted was to be close to John.

But that was all behind them now. They had managed to escape together. This was their new start. And they would have to find a way to leave their old lives behind.

She grinned at her husband as he circled back toward her. "They're showing up tomorrow? Then why don't we do some work today? We'll be too busy to let them get to us!"

She wished she felt as confident as she was trying to sound. When the Daltons arrived in town, anything was possible.

TWO

The New Jersey countryside sped by, mostly farmland now that they had passed the ugly sprawls of Newark and Trenton—and mostly shades of tan and brown in the February cold. It was still quite pretty in an austere, empty sort of way. The Mercedes was filled with the strains of Pachelbel's "Canon in D Minor." Ralph had invested in a state-of-the-art sound system especially for long trips like this. But Angela Dalton Sumner couldn't concentrate on either the passing scenery or the music swelling around her. Her thoughts kept returning to her brother John.

Sometimes, Angela thought her brother would never understand. If he could just compromise a little, everything would be fine. But he never saw it that way. He had to quit the firm—again!—and run off to the rock-bottom end of New Jersey, of all places.

As if their father, Thomas P. Dalton II, would ever let any of them truly get away. She had been summoned to his office the first thing this past Monday, the moment she had stepped through the front door. That sort of order always meant a bit of trouble, but she didn't realize how much until she saw her father. His face was cold, his voice totally devoid of emotion; a sure sign that he was extremely angry. He had gotten a report from one of those people he employed. John had actually taken his mother's money and was in the process of buying a small hotel—a bed-and-breakfast, really—down in a seaside resort, hours away from Manhattan. She was to go down there by week's end, to "bring things back in line."

Thomas P. Dalton would make sure he remained the master of everything he surveyed. And nothing upset him more than a challenge from a member of his own family—even from weak-willed, wrongheaded John. Angela had agreed to everything, of course. And when her all-powerful father was sure Angela would make things right, when the cold fury finally drained from his face, she had never seen him look so old.

Angela had spent the last sixteen years doing just this sort of thing for the firm—tying up loose ends for her father—bringing things in line—usually legally. Almost always the solutions involved substantial sums of money. It never mattered who or what. Angela stepped in as the company representative, and her father's problems disappeared. Her two brothers were hopeless, Tip, a financial whiz who liked nothing better than working alone, and John—well, she could see what happened to John.

Dear Daddy, struggling to maintain all the control he could over his swelling empire, over his fragmenting family, even as his own body began to let him down. In the last few months, his seventy-eight-year-old heart had seemed to want to take its own vacation, even if the old man didn't. What did the specialists call them? Episodes. Her father had had two of them. A third one—only a matter of time, the specialists agreed—might be fatal.

Why couldn't John be patient, like his brother and sister? Sooner or later, Thomas P. Dalton II's body would fail. Finally, when their father was dead, they could all do and have what they wanted.

And what did Angela want? She glanced at her husband, Ralph. He seemed so happy, driving this big, expensive machine. They probably hadn't exchanged a dozen words on the way down here. They had figured out, early in the marriage, that she wasn't much of one for small talk. Ralph was good about that. So long as he had her money, he didn't mind a few inconveniences.

Ralph didn't even care that, in her family's world, he would always be an outsider. The Daltons were tied together by blood. And the blood had grown thicker as their father had aged.

Angela stared at the passing sky, bright with winter cold. It was all their mother's fault. Emily Parington had been everything her father had ever wanted; born into money, accepted by society, quite beautiful in those early pictures of the two of them together, and, in those days, always smiling. Angela's father, successful as he was, had been looked down upon in certain quarters because he had pulled himself out of poverty. It didn't matter how much money he acquired. The dirt was still on his hands.

Thomas P. Dalton II had seen a partnership with Emily as a way to rise above his roots, and had dazzled her with the same energy he had learned to use on politicians and stockholders. The outcome was inevitable. They had married, a grand social event of their day, and probably the last happy moment the couple ever had.

Once Emily was securely in place, her new husband started to use her money and social position, and to push her further and further into the background. They still managed to have children, eldest son, Thomas III, better known as Tip, Angela two years later, and John, another six years further down the line, at what Angela now realized was her parents final attempt at reconciliation—an attempt that ended even before their youngest son was born. Angela's memories were mostly of Connecticut, with her Manhattan-based father visiting on weekends and holidays—then only on holidays—then hardly ever. Even to a girl in her young teens, it had felt more like an armed truce than a marriage.

But even armed truces had a way of ending. Thirteen years ago, Angela's mother had found out something about their father, something that actually frightened him enough to let her go.

In the end, Emily had almost gotten away, and their father could never forgive any of them for that.

Their parents were never officially divorced—no scandal for the Daltons—but they had lived separately for the last dozen years of their failed marriage. Angela had been in college by that time, and older brother, Tip,

had already started his career as part of father's firm.
Until then, that had been one of the family's unwritten
laws—Tip, Angela, and John were all to be a part of her
father's empire, while Emily stayed as a wistful "orna-
ment" just outside.

But the secret passed between her parents, and everything changed. John, the youngest, had gone to stay with
his mother, and lived away from his father during his
high school years. Angela supposed that was what fueled
John's rebellion. He wanted a distance from the family—
a distance granted by their mother—that their father
would no longer allow.

Their father could never forgive their mother, even
though she had been dead for close to two years. And
now he could never forgive John. Mother was in the
grave. But John would pay in her stead.

Not that her father would deal with the situation directly. No, he would send Angela as his enforcer. Not, of
course, that the family used that sort of language.

What were the last words her father had said on the
matter? After telling her to tie up the loose ends? Something like "Look out for John. Let's see that he doesn't
hurt himself."

The words almost sounded sympathetic.

It didn't matter. Angela knew exactly what he
meant. For the family's happiness, no—for her father's
satisfaction—John had to be brought back into the fold.

John could be difficult. He had quit the firm twice
before. Once, because he couldn't work with one of
their father's handpicked supervisors, Dick Buckley—
a bastard if there ever was one, but her father's kind of
bastard. The other time—so John claimed—over a matter

of ethics, as if their clients didn't exchange privileged information all the time. Both times Angela had coaxed him back into the fold, if the word *coaxed* could apply to the way they had ended up fighting.

She hoped this time John wouldn't be quite so difficult. Maybe she could appeal to him through his wife. Even at John's worst moments, Karen had seemed to be a peacekeeper, diffusing arguments between father and son, and sister and brother.

Marrying her was probably the best thing John had ever done—at least for the family. Even Angela considered Karen a decent-enough woman—a little weak maybe, but that was just like John. Everything else her brother did seemed to mess up big time. And not simply the repeated quitting. He had tried to start a business each time he left, and had gone in with a couple of college buddies on a third venture while still with the firm. All of them had gone down in flames within a year to eighteen months. John had had no alternative—every time—but to reinvest himself in the family firm.

Of course, Angela and their father had had a say—without John's knowledge—in some of those business dealings—including the sudden cancellation of a couple of separate contracts. Angela was very proud that she had kept John from finding out the truth about her involvement.

And John? Once he was back in the fold, like every time before, he would be fine—a credit to the firm—so long as he just sat and did as he was told. He always worked hard when he was with the company. A year would go by, maybe two. Then he always found a new reason to leave.

Their mother's will had just stirred up things best left buried, and she had found one final way to drive a wedge through the middle of the family.

But Angela would take care of that, too.

She looked up at the highway. Signs announced they were reaching the end of the Garden State Parkway. Oddly enough, it just petered out, the four lanes of the superhighway turning into the two lanes of a local road.

"We're getting close. Just a couple more lights, and we should be in town."

They had this end of the road more or less to themselves. Not much tourist business in the middle of February, and the locals were mostly busy in the middle of a workday afternoon. Everything was pretty flat out here, like it often was close to the ocean, and they passed by miles of fallow fields and marshland. For a minute, Angela felt she and Ralph and their car could drift forever through this silent, empty landscape, broken only by a few bare trees, the occasional distant house.

What was wrong with her? Angela shook her head. Maybe this was why John liked it out here. It didn't look much like New York City, or even like most of industrialized New Jersey. Even though they were still some distance from the Atlantic, she could feel that nature had a greater hold here than in the city, where she was comfortable. She had a sudden vision of herself standing out in one of those endless fields, waiting to be swept away, to vanish behind a gust of wind, a sudden storm, or maybe even the sea itself.

"Ralph?" she said, rather more loudly than she had intended. Still, it reassured her to hear the sound of her own voice.

Her husband quickly turned down the classical music. It was Vivaldi now, *The Four Seasons;* she hadn't even heard the music change as she had stared at the passing scenery.

"Something the matter, dear?"

His question made her think how foolish this all was. She quickly glanced down at the Triple A TripTik on her lap. "I thought we missed our turn," she said with a note of apology. "But I think it's still up ahead."

Ralph nodded. "Just let me know."

Houses appeared on either side of the road. They were finally entering Cape May. She saw a sign ahead, directing them to the commercial district.

"Turn here, Ralph."

They had left the fields behind and now passed copses of trees and clusters of homes, the occasional gas station and country store, a sort of civilization. As they drew closer to the ocean, Cape May began to grow around them, small summer cottages giving way to grander houses, built back when this resort was the place to be.

The road into town turned into Ocean Avenue, the main thoroughfare into town, and the street that held the Abbadon Inn. Angela thought she glimpsed the ocean, only a few blocks ahead. This part of town was downright charming. The streets were lined with well-preserved Victorian houses. She saw that her brother would have a bit of competition. From the signs out front, nearly every one of these grand old places had been transformed into a bed-and-breakfast. The buildings grew even grander closer to the Atlantic.

"Here!" Ralph called as they pulled to the curb

within a couple blocks of the sea, with an unobstructed ocean view. She looked where her husband pointed at a large, weathered sign:

THE ABBADON INN
1858

Behind it was a Victorian a bit larger than its neighbors. Location, location, location. This spot looked delightful even on a dreary February afternoon. The inn needed a coat of paint, but with a little work, it would look as charming as everything else on the street. She was surprised at her brother's taste and foresight. This might be an investment worthy of a Dalton.

"Then this is the place?" Ralph asked.

"I think so," she replied. Yet she didn't feel eager to get out of the car. Maybe she still felt a little uneasy about her reaction outside of town, or maybe she hadn't quite determined the best way to confront her brother. Every word she'd say would be important, especially now that she wanted to add this inn to the Dalton holdings.

She glanced at her husband. "I don't want to stop just yet. Let's drive around a bit, get a sense of the town, see what my brother has gotten into."

"A tour of the resort, hey?" Ralph shrugged. "You're the boss."

She was, wasn't she? She smiled as her husband drove her down to the beach. Her aging father, her two brothers, one who didn't want to grow up, the other so involved with numbers that he didn't want to deal with people—out of all the Daltons, Angela was the one who was all business. Maybe it took a little inn on the Jersey Shore for her to realize that. And maybe she could take this weekend not just to bring John back, but to make the others realize how valuable she was.

The doorbell didn't seem to work. Eddie Knox pounded on the door.

It swung open. A woman maybe five years younger than Eddie frowned out at him.

"Oh. Thank goodness," she said as soon as she saw him.

He laughed at that. "That's a better reaction than I usually get."

The woman smiled back at him. She was quite good-looking when she smiled. Tall, maybe five-foot-eight, and thin, with an oval face framed by dark brown hair. Nice cheekbones, nice eyes. Eddie realized he was staring. She looked away for an instant, but then she looked back again.

"We were expecting somebody else," she replied.

Eddie pulled his own gaze away to look at the doorway above her. "Undertakers?" he asked. "Tax collectors?"

"Family."

Eddie nodded, smiling in turn. "I moved down here to get away from mine."

"So did we. It didn't work." She flushed slightly, as if suddenly embarrassed.

Well. Eddie didn't like to make people uncomfortable. "Claire sent me, from Cape Realty," he quickly explained. "I'm Eddie Knox, from Knox Construction."

She nodded, once again at ease. "Oh, right. She said to expect you in the next couple days." She blinked, then added, "Oh. I'm Karen Dalton."

"Pleased to meet you." He nodded in return. "Well, I can't get in to finish my next job until the plumbers are done. It's only a block over from here on Gurney Street. That way." He pointed when he saw the questioning look on her face. "Anyway, I thought I'd stop on over here, see what you're looking for, maybe figure what I need to get started."

"That's great! Let me go get my husband."

Eddie nodded as she turned and left the doorway. That was the story of his life. The ones who were easy to talk to always had husbands. Well, she had said "we" early on—who else would she mean? The realtor had mentioned something about a couple, too, hadn't she? Come on, Eddie. Enough of the lonely-hearts. Back to work.

He took a step just inside the door and glanced around the lobby.

The place appeared to be in fairly decent shape. He knew it had been vacant for a while, but it looked like somebody had spruced it up a bit. Maybe he'd have to ask Claire and find out who else she used to do these little fix-ups. Well, he shouldn't be too nosy. She called him this time, and he wanted to stay on her good side. Knox Construction, seeing as it consisted entirely of Eddie and his cousin Stan, needed to get as much local work as possible.

Karen came back, leading a tall, thin man who seemed to be studying the floor. Karen tugged at his hand as they stopped.

"This is my husband, John," she said as the man looked up at Eddie. "This is the man Claire said would come over from Knox Construction."

"Eddie Knox," he repeated, holding out his hand. "Call me Eddie."

"You can call me John."

His handshake was reasonable, but he didn't have much of a smile. Eddie couldn't help but think John had something else on his mind. He seemed a little sad, as if life had already beaten him down. Outsiders looked a lot of things; happy wasn't one of them. Whenever Eddie saw some of these big-city people, he was glad he was just a carpenter in a small town.

"Well, this is a pleasant surprise," John continued, even though the look in his eyes said there was nothing pleasant about it. "It's good to know the folks around here are on their toes. I think there are a few things around here we need to get working."

Eddie pointed over his shoulder. "Like your doorbell."

"That, too?" John stared past Eddie at the door. His smile was gone.

"I'm afraid so. I gotta get the electricians in to do that, though. What all would you like done? I thought we could go over what you wanted done, work up some estimates. Maybe look at something I can start on right away."

John waved for Eddie to come in over the threshold. "Trust me, we have a list of things to do. We thought we'd get the kitchen fixed up first."

"It's always good to eat."

John didn't even smile at that. No sense of humor, apparently. Or the guy's mind was elsewhere. Maybe Eddie should cool it with the cheerful banter.

"Let's have a look at your kitchen, so we can see what you have in mind," he quickly said.

"It's right down here." John turned and walked down the hall. Eddie followed. John stopped in the middle of what would probably be the dining room, a long space that took up the back half of the first floor, as if he had forgotten something. The owner shook his head and began to walk again.

"I'm sorry," John called over his shoulder. "I've got things on my mind."

"Opening and running a place like this can be a big job," Eddie replied—his attempt to make peace. It was a true statement that probably had nothing to do with John's problems. Opening this kind of place was a huge job, in fact far bigger than most people thought. A lot of people had come down in the last dozen years or so, a pretty constant pilgrimage since Cape May was declared a national historic site. All of them had been sure they were going to slice a piece of the tourist pie. But that tourist pie was only fresh in the summer, and you had to keep these places going year-round. Maybe half of them made a go of it. Eddie had seen some of the new owners come and go in less than a year.

"Eventually, we want to get the restaurant going, too."

"So you're thinking ahead?" Eddie said to keep up his end of the conversation. They could probably put two dozen tables in this kind of space. "Well, more people are coming every year."

"That's what I hear."

Eddie didn't want to be too negative around somebody giving him work. There had been success stories, too. Down on the far side of the beach, a couple of

South New Jersey builders had put a lot of money into
Angel-by-the-Sea—a two-building complex that dwarfed
this hotel. Angel seemed to be pulling people in already.
And this place was much more centrally located. It
could probably be an even bigger success, once the
owner got an attitude adjustment.

Oh, hell. Maybe Eddie just met the guy on a bad day.
As long as folks like these kept pouring their money
into Cape May, Eddie would find work. That's as far
ahead as he wanted to think.

John led Eddie into the kitchen, another large space
with two huge ovens and a stainless-steel refrigerator—
the kind of grand old Victorian kitchen big enough for
the restaurant business. It had obviously already been
modernized at some point.

John pulled a yellow pad off the counter and handed
it to Eddie.

"Here. This is a preliminary list."

Eddie looked down at the top sheet, where, in neat
block lettering, someone had listed close to two dozen
different tasks.

Wow. If these folks could afford it, Claire had
handed Eddie a gold mine. This is what the real estate
folks called a "Fixer-Upper." There were no huge jobs
on the list, but the sheer bulk of two- and three-day jobs
would take Knox Construction months to complete. He
scanned through the listed tasks, which started on the
hotel's exterior, then worked their way inside through
the first, second, and third floors. They would have to
replace some of the exterior shingles, one corner of the
roof, and a couple of windows. Plus one of the chim-
neys was questionable. Eddie would have been tempted

to whistle—if he didn't think the owner would take it the wrong way.

Some of these things—especially the roof—would have to wait until the weather got a little better. You didn't want to lay down shingles when the temperature was this cold—they would never set right. They would have to start on the bottom of the list, about half of which seemed to center on the kitchen.

John sighed heavily. "We have a limited amount of money we can put into this."

Eddie nodded. Maybe it wasn't that much of a gold mine after all. "And you want to get people in here as soon as possible, so you can get some of that money back."

John nodded, grateful that Eddie understood.

"If you can prioritize what needs to be done, I can give you an idea of what everything will cost. We probably want to work mostly inside now, things people are going to see. And you want to start with the kitchen?"

John looked over the list himself, as if he was having second thoughts. With a list like that, even Eddie could get overwhelmed.

"Well," John said at last, "maybe the rooms upstairs first, but then the kitchen. At least enough to get it running."

Eddie walked farther into the kitchen to get a look around. The twelfth item on the list was "Replace kitchen wall." Just beyond the ovens, a whole section of the wall was pitted and black.

"What happened here?"

"The real estate agent said there had been a fire," John replied. "I don't know any more than that."

"Oh, yeah. I remember reading something about that." This was a fire all right. Odd that it showed here and not above the ovens. It seemed to Eddie that somebody had died in that fire, too. Funny that Claire hadn't mentioned that to the new owners.

Karen popped her head through the kitchen door. "So how's it going?" The room grew far warmer.

Her husband smiled. Maybe he wasn't a totally cold fish after all.

Eddie turned back to the task at hand. "So you want to patch this up, maybe replace the floor over here. This counter over here will have to be replaced, too. I bet we can match the tile."

Dust shook out as he tapped the blackened wall.

"This should be fairly easy to clear out. Sometimes, though, these old places surprise you."

"Do you think this can be done quickly?" John asked.

Uh-oh. The all-important time question. "Let me take a look." He got down on his knees to peer through where the fire had burned a hole. The damage didn't appear to be that extensive. But Eddie Knox knew you could never take these houses at face value. Once you started tearing into the walls, you never knew what you would find.

Generally, these old buildings had good, solid construction. Both labor and materials were relatively cheap in the late nineteenth century when these places were built, and they were designed by prominent architects, many imported from Philadelphia or New York. Problems usually came from what the later occupants had done to the places—it wasn't uncommon to find live wires hanging loose behind the walls, or to discover some home-handyman project had cut through a support beam or two.

The fire seemed to have been caught before it could do too much damage. The exposed beam looked a little singed but basically untouched. He ran his hand along the support, then rapped it with his knuckles.

What was this stuff? It looked like dark wood, but it felt more like stone. Good luck pounding nails into this baby. He wondered if this beam might have come from an earlier structure—it didn't look like anything else in the wall. Maybe, when they built the kitchen, they just built around it. Eddie supposed he could do the same, maybe box the beam with two-by-fours and build out from there. Pull the wall out a couple of inches and nobody would be the wiser. That was the true success story of Knox Construction. You just had to let some houses keep their secrets.

"Found anything terrible yet?" Karen asked.

"No worse than in any of these places." He looked at the edge of the fire damage, next to one of the ovens. The wall was separated from the stove by a three-foot patch of brick—probably part of a chimney, way back when.

A pounding noise was coming from the far end of the house. Eddie realized it must be someone at the front door.

"Excuse me," John said abruptly. "I'm expecting somebody else."

Karen looked after her husband, then back down at Eddie, as if she wasn't sure what she should do.

Eddie pulled out a piece of loose brickwork. A number of bricks seemed to have been cracked and split by the fire.

"We may have to replace some of these bricks."

He peered more closely at the space behind the crumbling mortar. "Wait a sec. There's something back here."

He pulled a few more bricks free—they came out all too easily—he would have to start his repairs here before part of this wall collapsed. He reached into the space behind—certainly an old, unused chimney—and brought out a small, olive green metal box, dented, scratched, and covered with a layer of dirt. He lifted it toward Karen. "I guess this is yours."

"Mine?"

Eddie grinned. "Hey, you buy one of these places, all the contents come with it."

He heard raised voices from the other room.

Karen looked toward the noise. "Oh, dear. Maybe I'd better go and see how John's doing."

Eddie guessed the family had arrived. Still holding the box, he rose to his feet.

"It sounds like you're going to be busy. Why don't I just let myself out through the back door? I've got a job or two I'm finishing up, but I should be free in a couple days. Maybe toward the end of the week."

Karen looked a bit flustered. She kept glancing toward the front of the house. "I'm afraid we don't have a phone number yet."

He fished a card from his shirt pocket. "Just give me a call when you do, and we'll get started." When it's a little quieter, he thought but didn't say.

She smiled gratefully.

"Take this, too." He handed her the box.

"Thank you, I guess," she said. She frowned briefly

as they heard her husband shout. She hastily placed the box in a cupboard and closed the door.

The voices rose even more in the other room. Maybe, Eddie thought, there was a good reason John was so gloomy.

Eddie nodded at the kitchen door. "I'll let myself out the back."

"Thank you," she replied. "I'll let John know what you said." She took a step to go toward the voices. "I'd better get out there."

Eddie had already opened the door leading outside. "Good idea. I'll talk to you soon."

The noise stopped as the door swung shut. He was glad he was out. He didn't need to listen to other people's arguments. He realized he was starting to like both of the Daltons—even sad John. Maybe they could make a go of it after all. Though it sounded like they needed to ditch their family first.

THREE

Angela was a little shocked by the look on her brother's face. When he was angry, his round face looked even more like their mother's. The lines on his forehead, the creases around his mouth, all looked like she had when Angela was a child and had done something wrong.

"What exactly are you doing here?" he asked as soon as he opened the door. He was livid, his voice an accusatory growl. None of the usual family niceties here.

Angela didn't know what to say. She hadn't expected John to be quite so direct.

"Well, hello to you, too," was what she finally decided on. She would smile, even if her brother would not.

John frowned down at her. He stood in the doorway, blocking the way in. She had often found John's stubbornness when he was angry amusing in the past. Before this, Angela had always been able to talk him out of it.

But that had usually been back in New York, on the Daltons' home turf. She was at something of a disadvantage here. She realized it was time to treat John a bit more seriously.

"We came down here to talk to you," she said softly.

"Whether I want to talk or not? You just can't give me any space at all."

No, Angela thought but didn't say, *unfortunately I can't. And we both know the reason why.*

"I didn't ask you to come here. I don't want you here." John's voice was growing louder. He was nearly shouting.

She heard Ralph walk up behind her. He had parked the car across the street.

"Hello, John," Ralph said affably.

Her brother nodded at her husband, his anger turned down a notch toward the new arrival.

"Hello, Ralph. I'm afraid you guys can't stay here."

Ralph tried to smile his way through his own confusion. "I'm sorry. I don't think we were actually planning—"

"John!" Angela cut her husband off. She decided to use the lull in her brother's anger to try the approach she had hit upon in the car. "We weren't expecting to stay with you. This is just supposed to be a friendly visit. We were so surprised when you bought this place. We wanted to congratulate you."

"We were curious," Ralph chimed in. "Always wanted to see Cape May."

"What do you mean by 'we'?" John asked, much more quietly than before.

She sighed. "You know Dad wants to know every-thing."

"I'm surprised how quickly he wants it, too," John added. "This is the first time I've ever seen you away from New York on a weekday."

"What do you mean?" Angela countered. "I get away." She glanced at her husband. Ralph had turned to study the neighborhood.

"Business trips, mostly," she admitted. Her brother had gotten her on the defensive. That was new, too. She might have to rethink her strategy.

"This is a business trip, too," John confirmed.

Angela wouldn't deny it. She had to find her way back to neutral territory.

"We can banter back and forth all day," she said in-stead. "Why don't we talk inside?"

"I don't think so." John shook his head. "Once you're inside, I don't think I'll ever get you out."

In a way, Angela realized he was right. But both she and her brother also knew the Daltons would all be a part of this property, or none of them would. That was the way of things, so long as their father ran the show.

She might as well say it out loud. "Nobody does anything in the Dalton family—alone. It's foolish to do anything by yourself. Not when you have our re-sources."

That just seemed to make John upset all over again. "I never wanted you here. I never even told anyone about this. How did you find out about this place?"

"You know," she replied.

"My father knows everything!" John was shouting

again. "My father owns everything. But my father doesn't own me. I resign from the family!"

"Nobody resigns from the family." Angela almost smiled at the absurdity of such an idea.

"Because of fucking Thomas P. Dalton the Second!" John shot back.

Ralph shuffled his feet uncomfortably. "Maybe I'll go wait in the car."

"We're just having a discussion here, Ralph," Angela snapped. "Give us a minute." She turned back to John. "Yes, Daddy knew. How? Even I don't know where he gets some of his information. His money talks."

"His money does a lot more than just talk!" John had gotten all wound up again. Angela wondered if there was any way of talking him back down.

"So we have visitors?" Karen showed up, standing just behind her husband. "I heard the voices."

How could she help but hear the voices? The way John was shouting, fishing boats out on the Atlantic could probably hear every word. But Karen's arrival seemed to have cut John off, mid-tirade.

Angela smiled at the newcomer. "Oh, Karen. So good to see you." Maybe his wife could calm John down.

"I don't think these are the best of circumstances," Karen replied without a smile of her own. "I'll be honest. I don't see why you need to be down here."

Angela decided to take another approach. "I don't think either of you are looking at the bigger picture. Maybe we could help out. A place like this will take a lot of work."

"What kind of work are you talking about?" Karen

looked very skeptical. "Are you going to help us sand the floors?

Ralph perked up. "We could rent a sander? That might be fun, actually."

Trust her dear husband to blunder into the middle of this. Angela kept her smile.

"Well, you know I'm not the floor-sanding type." She patted her well-coifed head with a manicured hand. "But seriously. This might be a bigger project than you can handle by yourself."

"You're talking money here?" Karen asked.

They were finally getting down to basics. "In the Dalton family, we're always talking money."

"So I've learned." Karen shook her head. "I'm sorry. It's too early for this conversation. We only got the keys to this inn today. We've literally just gotten our feet inside the door. We have no idea how much we want to do. And there's no way to discuss it with you, even after John and I have talked. We don't even have a phone yet."

But Angela wasn't going to let them get away that easily. "There are other places to talk. Let the Dalton money take you out to dinner."

John looked disgusted at the very idea, but Karen hesitated. She looked at her husband. "This inn is ours. There is no way they are taking it away from us. I suppose we could let them talk."

"Look," Angela added quickly, "you know our father won't quit until he has a hand in this. But it doesn't have to be much of a hand. We can work it out so Dad only thinks he has control."

"You'd do something like that?" John asked. "Let

us—what—work out some sort of token association with the company, and then leave us alone?" His voice rose again. "What exactly are you offering here?"

"Well, if we can discuss it—inside someplace?" Angela looked up and down the street. "Maybe we can talk about this so that all the neighbors don't know all our business."

Ralph looked up the street. "Are there even neighbors this time of year? I parked right across the street."

Karen smiled at that. "We don't know. We haven't met a soul. Like I said, we just got here."

It looked like nobody knew much of anything. Maybe, Angela realized, that was a good place to start.

"Look, John. We haven't always fought. Back when we were kids, we used to put up a united front against Dad's craziness. Remember that time, when Dad tried to punish Tip by not giving him dinner, and we all refused to eat?" She found the memory particularly refreshing. Life was so much simpler when they were kids. "Dad has found a way to set us up against each other, hasn't he? But all that sort of thing is waiting back in New York. We're in a new place here. Maybe we can go back to the way we used to be, before the company got in the way. Maybe we can find a new way to work together. Maybe we can screw with our father's head all over again."

"This sounds a little like the Angela I used to know a long time ago. My smart-mouthed big sister." John started to grin back at her. He looked like he didn't really believe what was coming out of his own mouth. He glanced at his wife, then back at his sister. "I'll take this one step at a time. If you're willing to wait until tomorrow, we can talk."

Angela worked quickly to close the deal. The four of them would find someplace open for lunch and talk at noon tomorrow.

John and Karen quietly closed the door, and Angela and her husband walked back to the car. They had reservations at one of the large hotels across from the beach. They could check in, and, after she had made some calls, spend the rest of the day doing something else. It could almost be like a vacation. And on a weekday.

Angela was amazed. Things had come out of her mouth back there that she had thought but not said for a long time. She knew there had to be some way to get to her brother—she had expected to use money, threats, emotional manipulation.

She never expected she would use honesty.

Karen was surprised at how well things had gone. Brother and sister had actually come to an agreement in a matter of minutes. Maybe, even if they couldn't find common ground about John's father and the company, they could find a way to talk. It would be so much easier on John if he had an ally inside the family.

John closed the door and turned away from Karen. He paced into the front room.

"I have to get out of here," he said as he faced the far wall.

"John? I thought we handled that pretty well."

He stopped and turned around to look at her. "As well as we could, I guess. It still drives me crazy. The way my sister says one thing one day, then completely turns it around the next. She actually sounded sincere."

"It's your family." Karen sighed. She didn't think she had ever seen Angela this open. But she had seen the Daltons break promises before, too. She remembered all the plans she and John had had when they were first married, plans encouraged by her father-in-law, eager to see his son settled down and wed. Of course, once the marriage was done, John's father saw no reason to extend himself further. John hadn't gotten anything on paper, had he? They would have to discuss it some other time when his father was free. And his father was never free. Promises of support vanished, and John was folded back into the company under his father's control.

"It's my family," John agreed. "And apparently I'm going to have to work with them, whether I want to or not. Why can't they leave me alone?"

Karen didn't bother to answer.

"We don't see them till tomorrow," John continued. "I gave us a day. There's something Angela isn't telling us. They always start the dance nice and sweet before they stick in the knife."

Karen had seen this time and again. John would let the sourness overtake him again, close in on himself. There was nothing that John's family could do to him that he couldn't do much more quickly to himself.

Karen didn't want to watch that all over again. This hotel was their chance—maybe their last chance. She had to keep John positive and involved if they were going to hope to make a go of it.

"Maybe something different is going on here. You know, your dad is getting on in years. What is he—seventy-five? Seventy-six? Maybe Angela is looking for what's going to happen after he's gone."

John didn't reply. As old as his father was, Karen knew he still came across like some force of nature. Even Karen thought he'd live forever.

"I don't even think it matters if my father's in the picture anymore," John said after a moment. "They'll find a new way to undercut me. They always do."

"Your family bought us this place."

"You mean my mother did."

"The mother who raised all of you. Angela, too. She cared about you."

"Maybe, a little bit. But she really did it as a final way to get back at my father."

As much as she wanted to argue, Karen was afraid that John was right. Nothing was simple between the Daltons. It tore John apart. Karen was afraid it would tear their marriage apart as well.

John looked past Karen, at the door. "I have to go out, walk the beach for a while."

"Would you like me to come along?"

"No. I've got to sort things out for myself." He looked back at his wife. "I know we've got things to do. I'll only go out for a little while."

"Fine. Remember, we went into this B-and-B business together. And we'll get through it together. I'll think about this some, too. Tonight, when we go out to dinner, let's come up with what we want to say—and what we don't want to say—to your sister."

John actually smiled at that. "What? And take away her ability to blindside us? It sounds like a good idea."

He kissed her gently on the forehead. "We really are in this together, huh? I'm awfully lucky to have found you."

She squeezed his arm in return. "From now on, we're both going to be lucky."

"From now on," John said as he went to retrieve his winter coat, "we're going to plan ahead, and leave nothing to chance."

She really hoped that could be so.

John waved as he walked out the door.

FOUR

Karen leaned against the counter in the lobby, feeling as empty as the room before her. John had left to work out his demons, leaving her alone in the project that already seemed to consume their lives. They had come here to rid themselves of the complexities of Manhattan. She sighed. This place might be bare, but it wasn't simple.

She almost laughed. What exactly were they looking for in Cape May? Something pure and simple like running an inn out by the sea? Pure and simple and romantic, and probably totally unrealistic.

She stared at the faded wallpaper in the lobby. When the real estate agent had first shown them around, every room had looked so full of promise. Now everything looked weathered, sad, and old. Rather than a way to bury their problems, she was afraid this place would bring them all up out front, like walls that would separate John and Karen forever.

No. She wouldn't give in to negativity. She thought of all the plans they had made—how many guest rooms could they open quickly (their guess was nine)—what to do with the kitchen (start by serving breakfast, perhaps open the restaurant with a limited menu sometime in the summer)—even what color to paint the place (they'd agreed on a subdued blue, with a red-and-gold trim).

Maybe they didn't really want simple. Maybe they really wanted different. Something the two of them could do together; a challenge that was theirs alone.

They would come up with a plan. Some new approach to take with John's family. Angela had already been surprised by their resolve. They had broken through her professional veneer—if only for a minute—to something underneath. It was the first time Karen had ever heard Angela sound—sincere. Maybe they could find a way to reach that part of her again.

Deep down, Karen had hopes for John, hopes for their marriage. When they could find a way to talk, things could be good. If John could get by his self-recriminations, his anger at himself and his family, he and Karen could really connect. She wouldn't let his father rub John's nose in his failures. All those were past. They were now somewhere new, and would be doing things on their own terms.

She hoped she could help make it happen. She didn't want to go back to where they were before this whole Cape May adventure began. Their marriage had been nothing but fights, then. John would lash out at her when he was really angry at his family. She would always break down in tears. Sometimes, they would both cry, as if they wanted desperately to touch each other but had forgotten how.

But this inn was really new. This was the start their marriage had never had. And how did they spend their first day here?

John had left her alone again.

Karen shook her head. Maybe John wouldn't change. Maybe she was just trying to find a reason to stay. She just didn't know anymore.

She wasn't going to solve anything by standing here and letting her thoughts run in circles. She should get started somehow, John or no John. What was the best way to introduce herself to the new inn?

She had that box that the carpenter had found—what was his name? Eddie? She hoped the rest of the locals were as easy to talk to. It would make a big difference if they could get to know their neighbors and be a part of someplace.

But that metal box was waiting for her. She hadn't had a chance to look at it—what with the argument raging at the front door. With luck, the box would have something of the inn's history. She could tell John about it and get his mind off his family. Well, unless the box was empty, or full of old bills or something. She'd keep the disappointment to herself.

Why didn't she look inside it first and see what it had to offer? She walked quickly back to the kitchen and pulled the box out of the cupboard. She cleaned it off. On the top was a faded label that read "Property of Jack Cooney."

It was closed with a single metal clasp, but the clasp was a little rusted and slightly bent. It didn't want to open with just the pressure of her fingers. So it would be a bit of a challenge? Karen was always up to a challenge.

She started to pull open drawers. If the former tenants left some pans behind, they probably left other things as well.

In the third drawer, she found an old iron knife, not very sharp. The blade had turned a dull reddish gray. She figured it was still sharp enough to give her some leverage. She worked the knife under the clasp, then slowly pulled the blade away from the box.

The clasp popped open with a satisfying *clack*. Karen smiled as she put down the knife. Just have to have the right tool for the job. She lifted the lid to get a look at the contents.

The box was full of yellowed papers. Perhaps not as exciting as jewelry or a treasure map. Well, she couldn't really rule out that map—at least not yet. She picked up the bundle and flipped quickly through them.

They looked to be letters, all written in the same hand. All dated from the early sixties. There were close to twenty letters here, dated over a period of close to a year. A year in the history of the Abbadon Inn. Sort of like her own private time capsule.

Why were these hidden behind a loose brick in the kitchen wall? Someone had secrets to keep, she guessed. Someone who had never bothered to retrieve them—or could not, for some reason. Someone must have left them there to be forgotten between one renovation and another. Without the nearby fire that had taken out part of the wall, even the carpenter wouldn't have known they were there.

Maybe this was an omen—a good omen—that she and John were supposed to be here. She'd look at these letters, see if there was anything to them, anything that might help them with the inn.

Maybe these could be an inspiration, and Karen and John could write something of their own—a diary perhaps. Maybe she and John could start their own little bit of history.

She looked at the letters again. They were neatly sorted by date. Well, why not start at the beginning?

She removed the first letter and unfolded the sheets of paper. Three of them, written on both sides, in a precise hand—probably a man's. She spread the pages out before her on the counter and began to read:

May 26, 1961

Dear Lucy,

> *The shore was alive tonight.*
> *My bosses gave me one of my rare nights off, so I decided to take a drive, get a whiff of the springtime air. I always drive by myself now. It's not at all like it was with you. That seems like a whole different world.*
> *I drove straight out of town and on to the back-country roads. That's the way I always do it these days. I don't pay much attention to where I'm going. I just want to be gone. But once you're in this*

kind of life, my kind of life, there's no way to get away. I remember how you tried to warn me about that, when we first met. I wanted to leave, then, but I couldn't, even for you. Even then, I think it was already too late.

I didn't know where I was going, but I knew what was behind me. I wanted to get out of town, away from people. And not just the boss and the boys. We'd gone though a long winter together, getting this hotel back in shape, and now that weather is getting better, it's a relief just to get outside, to stretch my legs, and get away from the others for an hour or two. But Cape May changes in the spring. The tourists start to trickle in. The tourist traps open along the beach. The bars start to get crowded on Saturday nights. Those winter walks when I would barely see a soul are long gone.

It's Saturday, and people are everywhere. I'm getting a taste of what it is going to be like during the summer. They say Cape May is ready for a big comeback, maybe it will get as big as it was before the war, or even back in the twenties, when people had money.

I guess that's what Tito is counting on. He wants to make Cape May the kind of destination it used to be way back when, full of all the wealthy folks from Philadelphia, New York, even Washington. The richer they are, the better. He wants to relieve them of all that heavy cash.

Today was a perfect, sun-filled Saturday, too, the first one we'd had after three weekends of April showers pushing their way into May. A lot of peo-

ple had apparently been waiting for this sort of
weather. It actually surprised me to see all the people out along the beach, walking up and down the
street. It was way too crowded. I had come to prefer
the empty, quiet streets of winter. That's not at all
the way I used to be. They used to call me Good
Time Cooney back in the Army—anything for a
party, the crazier the better. Not anymore. If I can't
have you, maybe I want everything else to be empty.

What the hell. That sort of feeling is too much
for me to think about tonight. I wanted life to be
simple. Just me behind the wheel, the windows
open, the air blowing in my face. I drove away
from the town, down to the point by the light-
house, and found a place away from everything
but a strip of trees and a broken-down dock.

I killed the lights and got out of the car. I
wanted just to listen to the water and look at the
stars. But even that wasn't going to happen tonight. As soon as the engine was quiet, I heard another sound, a shuffling maybe, no, more like a
clicking noise, like shells or stones dropped one
atop another.

It only took me a second to realize I wasn't
alone at all. As my eyes adjusted to the moonlight,
I saw that the whole beach was moving.

By trying to escape one crowd, I had stumbled
on another. Life has a million ways to make things
complicated.

I walked carefully out toward the sand, and
saw the moving shells, some the size of a fist,
some as big as a hubcap, crawling over each

other as they clambered out of the bay—horse-shoe crabs. There must have been a thousand of them, crawling over each other, pushing their way out onto the beach.

Have you ever seen these things? They look like something from another world, like shields full of sharp edges, made out of ancient, blood-red bones. And they do come from another world—a world before any of us in so-called civilization were even here. I walked over to the library and looked it up today. The horseshoe crab has been doing this for 360 million years.

Think about it—these harmless, evil-looking creatures were around with the dinosaurs, and maybe even before the dinosaurs. And every year, for a thousand times a thousand years, they have climbed onto this same beach to lay their eggs, ignoring the lone stegosaurus or woolly mammoth or human being that stood there watching. And when all the people are gone, the horseshoe crabs will still be climbing that beach. There are things out here—out where this little strip of land meets an ocean that seems to go on forever—that make you feel small. On this one night, every single year, the horseshoe crabs come in to lay their eggs—an impulse as old as time itself.

Everything changes. Things go on without us. We're only here for a minute, and then we're gone. But stuff like this goes on forever. That's what happened to me, out there underneath the stars. I thought about how old the world was, and how small we were inside it.

*Who decides who lives and dies? Everything
brings me back to thinking of you. I wish I could
come back for you. I wish you had never had to
leave. I wish so many things.*

*Maybe I think too much. I know I've done
things that were unforgivable.*

I still wish I could be with you.

Enough for now. I'll write again.

All my love.

It was signed "Jack."

What a strange letter. And what was this about "the
boss and the boys" and somebody named Tito "wanting all the money"? Apparently, the old inn held some
secrets.

She had gotten a storyteller here. And someone who
had lived in this inn. And, oddly enough, a man called
"Jack"—another form of her husband's name. Another
John.

She placed the letter back in the envelope, the envelope back in the box, and the box in the cupboard. All
nice and tidy. And private. For some reason, private was
important right now. Maybe she was reacting as much
as John to the Daltons' intrusiveness.

Karen wondered if she should tell John about the letters. Not yet. These seemed like her special find. These
letters could be her little vacation from real life. Lucy
and Jack—a story of a love gone for a quarter of a century. Unless the two of them had gotten together, perhaps
married, even settled in Cape May? They could be their

next-door neighbors. Maybe the other letters would tell the rest of the story.

An old-fashioned love story. Maybe it would give her some pointers for her real life. Resorts were always good for romance. Maybe Cape May could work the same charm.

So why not tell John? Was she still that mad at him?

Yes, maybe she was. Maybe she needed something that had nothing to do with John, or any of the Daltons.

Maybe she was just being foolish.

She walked out of the kitchen. *Enough of these old letters.* She needed to get to work.

The hotel felt very large, and cold, and empty.

She hoped John came back soon.

FIVE

Angela gazed out at the flat, gray sea. A fine, misting rain deposited tiny water drops against the glass. The hotel had given them a very nice room, with a large sliding door that led out to a balcony facing the ocean. Not that you would want to open the door on a day like this.

She had put in a phone call to the office, but, as usual, her father had not been available. Ralph had gone down to use the indoor pool, but Angela knew she had to stay behind. To her father, this report was the priority.

It was only mid-afternoon, but it felt as though she had been here for days. She didn't bother with the TV—afternoon talk shows and soaps bored her. She had brought a briefcase full of reports to review, even a big fat novel she had always meant to read. She found herself staring at the ocean and the rain.

Usually, she was coolly efficient. Never a moment

wasted. Things were different here. She had fallen out of her rhythm, cut off from her normal world by the sea and the storm. She didn't feel quite herself, as if her clothes, her hair, even her skin belonged to a stranger.

The rain beaded on the glass.

She kept thinking about her brother John. More than just her brother. For the first time in years, she was letting herself think about her family. How her older brother, Tip, had lost himself in a world of numbers. How reserved their mother had been when their father was in the house, and how much more their mother smiled when he was gone. How all three of them, Tip and Angela and John, had joked and fought—and talked—before their father's business world had swallowed them whole.

The icy rain made tiny popping sounds as the wind pushed it against the patio door. Behind it all, she could hear the faint sound of the ocean far below, the waves pushing in and out, in and out.

The phone rang. She blinked, startled to find herself sitting on a hotel bed. She reached over and picked up the phone.

"Angela!" It was her father. His familiar bark made even her name sound like an order. Enough of the ocean and the rain. It was back to business.

"Dad," she replied.

"You saw John?"

She told him that she had.

"Has he given up this foolishness?"

She hesitated an instant before she replied. "John never gives up easily. Besides, I think he might be on to something down here."

"Explain."

"This property. I think there's room for investment in Cape May. I've just started to look into it, but I believe the Daltons can make a profit from this."

"Really?" That was exactly the sort of thing her father always wanted to hear. "John's going to do something that'll make money?"

Angela paused again. She was playing a hunch here—she shouldn't commit to anything until she had really looked at the possibilities. "I'm not sure that he can, working with a single property. But if we could combine his venture with a couple more I'm considering, we could really have something."

"Is John ready to play ball on this?"

"It's a delicate operation. You know John."

That wasn't a positive enough response for Thomas P. Dalton II. Her father made a noise that was half a laugh, half a grunt of dismissal. "We can make him—" he began.

Angela cut him off. "Give me a couple days. John will be ready."

"Sounds like you've got things under control. I need you to be my eyes and ears. I can't concentrate when this sort of nonsense is going on. And there's some questions from the home office—a couple more things I need you to check on—"

His voice cut off abruptly.

"Dad? Dad?"

The phone line had gone dead. She clicked the button on the cradle but couldn't even get a dial tone, only a faint hiss, as though the wind had pushed its way into the telephone wires.

Angela frowned. The storm must be messing with the lines. Here, it was just rain, but inland, away from the ocean, it was probably ice and freezing rain. She looked back out at their floor-to-ceiling view. Everything was gray now, like some faded photograph. The cement boardwalk, a pair of shuttered buildings, the sand, and the sea. You could imagine you were here twenty, fifty, maybe even a hundred years ago.

She put the phone receiver back down in its cradle. The call had served its purpose. Her father had learned enough before the phone went dead. She was quite sure there were investment opportunities around here. She had no idea what they were. She had said that to give herself some time to figure out what she really wanted to do.

She had seen that John might have a chance to be independent, to be happy. And she realized she wanted to give him the room to do so. She wanted time for John. That surprised her a bit.

And she wanted time for herself, too.

The windows rattled with a new burst of wind. She saw tiny bits of white amid the raindrops.

Angela wondered if she could be happy, too.

She glanced at her watch. It would be getting dark soon. Ralph would come back from his swim, they'd get dressed and go out to dinner. Cape May had a number of fine restaurants, and the concierge had recommended one that was open year-round, a seafood place with a bit of a French flair. They would stop at a local wine shop on the way—the local zoning peculiarities meant that many of the restaurants were "dry," and you had to bring your own. But that meant they could pick one of their favorites. How long had it been since she and Ralph had

had a simple, relaxing meal, away from the grasp of Dalton Investments?

She was keeping things from her father. She was defying her father. She had lied to her father.

These days, the all-powerful Thomas P. Dalton II relied far too much on his underlings. As the years went by, he spent more and more time in Manhattan, less on the road. Angela didn't think he had left the city in the past eighteen months. As age took his edge, he was keeping close to what was familiar.

There were a lot of things she could hide from her father now.

She stared back out the window. The rain swept the beach as the light drained from the sky.

The small light by the bed looked very bright. The outside world was lost to the night. Angela stared at the glass and only saw her own reflection.

"See? It's open! What did I tell you?"

"I don't know, Kenny."

Kenny hit J.J.'s shoulder. It didn't really hurt through his dad's old peacoat. Plus, J.J. had expected it.

"You spaz! You never know anything! There's new people here, I tell you. I heard them yelling at each other just this morning!"

"Wow. They were fighting the day they moved in?" J.J.'s mom and dad usually saved it all up for Friday nights.

Kenny grinned, showing off the chipped tooth he had right up front. "They didn't even move in. My mom says they just bought the place."

J.J. still wasn't sure. "But what if they catch us going through their basement?"

Kenny made a pretty wet-sounding raspberry. "Nobody's home!" He pushed the door to the cellar open again. "Besides, they didn't even lock it! You don't lock the basement door, anything can get down there."

J.J. stared at the dark space beyond the doorway. "What are we looking for if nobody's moved in?"

"Hey, you never know what the last people left behind." Kenny grabbed J.J.'s shoulder and pushed him forward. "Get going, you turd!"

J.J. lost his balance, stumbling down the slate steps. How old were these stairs, anyway? He ducked his head as he half jumped, half fell into the basement of the old inn.

J.J. blinked, trying to get used to the darkness. The small, dirty windows hardly let in any light at all. He heard Kenny clamber down the steps behind him.

"Jeez!" Kenny yelped. "Will you look at this place."

Everything down here was gray or muddy brown, and covered with inches of dust. The floor was packed dirt, with a couple of large dark spots. Probably leftover stains from something. A huge old furnace took up one corner of the room. J.J. could see flickers of flame through the heavy iron grate. Just past the furnace was an old set of wooden steps leading up into the inn. Another corner held a gray, rotting workbench with some rakes and stuff leaning against it. The room was pretty small, maybe the size of J.J.'s kitchen. Why did a place as big as the Abbadon Inn have a basement this small?

"Whoa!" Kenny shouted in his ear. "Look at this! Behind you!"

J.J. spun around, expecting the worst.

He saw a dark space just below the ceiling, three feet top to bottom, extending along the entire wall of the cellar. It went back quite some ways, far beyond where the light would reach. This, J.J. realized, was the rest of the basement. Kenny had already thrust his arms in there, feeling his way around.

"Is there something in there?" J.J. asked.

"Yeah! It's some kind of storage space. This is where they'd keep all the good stuff!" Kenny leaned forward to peer inside. He was all ready to climb up and in.

"Wait a sec!" J.J. yelled. "You can't see anything in there!"

It seemed awfully dark in that space. You couldn't even see the walls on either side. Who knew how deep it was? It could go on forever.

"Jeez, you are such a girl!" Kenny complained. "I shoulda brought Ricky T. instead!"

"Nah!" J.J. shook his head violently, trying to stand up for every inch of his twelve-year-old boy opinion. "You said it! Anything can come down here."

"What d'you mean?" Kenny pulled his arms out of the hole.

"It's an abandoned basement. Things come down here in the winter. There could be a skunk or something!"

"A skunk?" That made even Kenny take a step away from the darkness. He walked toward the middle of the room like that was what he had wanted to do all along. "Maybe next time we can bring a flashlight. Look at this!" He rushed over to the workbench and grabbed the longest of the handles leaning there. He swung it out in front of him.

"This is one of those big cutting things! Like that guy at New Year's carries."

"A scythe," J.J. added. He shrugged. "My uncle's got one—the one who has the farm."

Kenny swung it a couple more times. "I bet we could really slice something with this." The long handle banged against the leg of the workbench. The blade of the scythe was red with rust. Bits of it shook away as dust flew from the wood.

"Not in that shape," J.J. was glad the scythe was falling apart. He would just as soon not find anything too sharp down here.

"Hoo-ha!" Kenny swung the thing again, banging the scythe against one of the stone-and-mortar walls. The blade snapped away from the wood with a dull clang.

Kenny stopped to stare at what he'd done.

"You're gonna break everything!" J.J. wished they could get out of here.

"Hey. Cool out! No one's ever gonna know we were here." He glanced up toward the ceiling. "Unless there's something better upstairs."

J.J. blinked.

"Kenny? You say something?"

It felt like somebody had whispered in his ear.

"What's the matter now, jerk-off?" Kenny dropped the broken scythe in the dirt. "If there's neat stuff down here, there's probably a lot more up there. Just there for the taking!"

"Quiet!" J.J. said. He heard it again. Where was it coming from? He couldn't make out the words.

"Hey, you know what my mom says when it's time

for dinner? Come and get it!" Kenny laughed like that was the funniest thing in the world.

The whispering was all around him now. J.J. waved at Kenny.

Kenny's mouth snapped shut before he could say anything else. He frowned and nodded like he heard it, too.

Kenny pointed to the dark empty space on the other side of the cellar.

The voice was coming from the dark. J.J. heard it, a little louder now as he took a step toward the hole. The sound rose and fell, close one second, then very far away. Maybe things echoed off these old walls. Could he see something in there? J.J. squinted. Did he see a light? No, two tiny lights, pinpricks, really, deep in the hole, like eyes that stared and never blinked.

Kenny started to walk toward the darkness, but J.J. wanted to back away. The voice never stopped. If only he could make out the words.

The whispering rose again, like a chill breeze touching his neck. J.J. knew what it was saying now.

"Jimmy." No one had called J.J. that since he was four.

"Kenny."

It was calling them both by name. The voice chuckled—it was not a happy sound—before it whispered four more words.

"Come and get it."

SIX

"My guess is this was more than you wanted to do at one time." Eddie grinned apologetically.

John and Karen both looked at the numbers spread out before them. Karen knew it was the final number that shocked them both: sixty-five thousand dollars.

Eddie had itemized everything. And—Karen knew from last year, when they'd done repairs to their loft— he was only charging maybe half the going rate for the same sort of work in New York. Before she had seen this, she hadn't realized the true scope of the repairs.

John coughed. "Well. We'll have to review everything."

"It looks reasonable enough," Karen countered. She didn't want to alienate the man before he even started. "It does look like a lot more when you break down every job."

"You're new to this sort of thing." Eddie shook his

head. "Starting up an inn, a B-and-B—whatever you want to call it—is gonna give you no end of surprises." He shuffled his feet as he glanced at the crowded room behind them. "Maybe I shouldn't have sprung this on you at dinnertime. But this weather was so lousy, I had a chance to work up the figures and brought them along to review."

"And we showed up for dinner," Karen added.

"Yep. Here you were." He shrugged. "This is the place everybody eats, in the winter at least. See? You're almost locals already."

"Well," John said as he closed the folder that contained all the paperwork—and all the numbers. "We should get our phone in tomorrow. We'll give you a call."

"Sounds good. Enjoy the rest of your meal." The contractor nodded to both of them with a final smile as he turned and walked back across the room.

"Well," John said again as he looked at Karen.

"Oh, dear," was Karen's reply.

John waved at the folder. "We can't do half of this. I had no idea—"

"No," Karen cut him off. "We both knew we couldn't do everything. We might have been a bit naïve about how much everything would cost."

"We'll just have to prioritize." He glanced down the list. "I guess those private bathrooms will have to wait."

"I'm sure we can still do some of the really important stuff—the absolute minimum before we can bring in paying guests."

John frowned and shook his head. But he was looking straight at Karen. And they were talking. That was a good thing about shock. It had taken them out of their funk. They both looked down at their half-eaten dinners. Neither one of them made a move toward their plate. Karen no longer had an appetite. But at least they were talking.

All afternoon, ever since John's sister arrived, there had seemed to be a wall between them. Or maybe the wall had been around John. Even when he came back from his walk, he wasn't really there. He would start to stay something, stop abruptly, and leave the room.

The only thing they had been able to agree on all day was to go out for dinner. And once it was finally time to go, Karen was glad to take the six-block walk despite the rain. They had decided to eat at a local pub, a restaurant a few blocks from the inn, and a place that, unlike most of its neighbors, was open year-round. According to their realtor, the food was good, and even better, relatively cheap.

The pub was close to full when they arrived, even with the storm raging outside. It looked like the same sort of place you could find up and down the East Coast, subdued lighting, wooden booths with red checkered tablecloths, a dartboard hanging between two neon beer signs. A couple of fish hung on the wall, too, to show they were close to the ocean. The hostess had shown them to an empty booth in the far corner of the room. John had slid in on one side, Karen the other.

John had smiled at her then, tentatively—a sort of peace offering, she guessed. Maybe, away from the inn, they might be able to unwind again. Karen had sighed. These last few weeks had been so wonderful. How they talked about the inn, their lives, their dreams—everything. She didn't want to lose that again.

They had quickly gotten their food. Everything seemed to relax a bit.

"Hey, is Cape May a small town or what?" a voice had called from just past Karen's shoulder. They were both startled to find the contractor they'd seen only that afternoon.

They had exchanged some small talk. And then Eddie had shown them the papers.

Now it seemed that John couldn't look at anything else. Karen watched her husband for a minute before she said the name both were avoiding.

"We are going to have to bring Angela in on this, aren't we?"

John nodded. "I guess we'll be going out and having a meal with them after all. I don't think we need to show her any of this, though."

"We don't want her to know how much we need the money?"

"Exactly. Look—back there at the inn—even I'll admit Angela sounded a little different. But that doesn't mean we have to tell her everything." He shook his head. "We'll wait and see how many strings come with every dollar."

Karen nodded. "Sounds like a plan." She never thought she would look forward to another crisis, but it felt as though they were working together again.

John pushed his plate away.

"You want any dessert?"

Janet Frost swept the steps. The storm had pushed all sorts of things into her yard. It was good to keep up appearances, even though there wasn't that much business this time of year.

She knew it was curiosity keeping her out here. She had spent the better part of an hour puttering about in her yard. It was a far nicer day than the day before, reaching into the mid-forties with the sun peaking through the clouds, but it was still February. But she couldn't quite bring herself to go indoors.

She wanted to get a better look at her new next-door neighbors, the owners of the Abbadon Inn. They hadn't come back to the place all day, as far as she knew. She had heard some sort of argument the day before—just as she and her family had returned from a shopping expedition. It was a hard thing, opening and running one of these places. She hoped the new couple didn't tear themselves apart; hoped they had better luck than the last couple who tried with the place. She shook her head. All these old houses were a lot of work. But some places seemed like they didn't want to be fixed up at all.

She looked around the yard, everything spic-and-span at last. Perhaps it was time to check back in on her son. That was the other reason she had come outside. She had thought it best if the house was quiet while J.J. rested. She had never seen the boy so upset. The way he had run into the house, white as a ghost; the way he couldn't say anything except "Mom—mom," over and over. After a while he had started to shake.

Janet had held him tight until the shaking had passed. She'd asked him what was wrong then. He'd muttered something about Kenny—no surprise to Janet. If anything had gone wrong, that boy was sure to be involved.

She had sat with him for a while then, reading some

passages aloud from *Science and Health* that she thought
would sound comforting. Depend on Mrs. Eddy; faith
could heal anything.

J.J. had finally drifted off to sleep. She had tucked
him in and come outside, confident that, if her son woke
and needed her, he could find her. She wanted to keep
her hands busy, and not think too much about that
Kenny Radcliffe.

She wondered for a minute if Kenny had gotten as
scared as her son. For all she knew, Kenny could have
caused whatever happened to J.J. She wouldn't put it
past the little brat.

Janet made a noise deep in her throat. Why was she
even worried about the other boy? If anything had really
happened to Kenny, his mother would have called her
up and given Janet an earful. Of course, that meant
Kenny's mother had to be home. Not to mention sober.
It would probably be a miracle if she was both.

Now, now, Janet chided herself. It was not for her to
judge.

She chewed a bit on her lower lip—a bad habit, she
knew. She should have put her foot down, told J.J. not to
see Kenny anymore. It wasn't as though J.J. didn't have
other friends. He was a popular boy, good at sports, and
doing well enough at school. But he was getting to that
age—near thirteen—when kids wanted to test their limits. Kenny was a fair-weather friend at best. He and J.J.
had been buddies a couple years ago, but Kenny had
dropped her son for boys that were a little older that
Kenny had found more exciting. Janet had been glad of
that. Kenny had been a little wild, even at ten.

But now, since Christmas, Kenny had returned. They

had found themselves in the same homeroom in middle school and had begun to talk again. They had gotten together on a Saturday, then a couple of weekends after that. Janet had been afraid of making too big a deal about Kenny. If she objected too much, J.J. would only find him more exciting.

This week, though, they had seen each other almost every day. It was the time of year. The dregs of February. Kids never had enough to do. Especially on school-vacation week. So she had kept her mouth shut. She figured once school started up again, the two would drift apart, and her worries would be done.

She had never seem J.J. so upset. *That Kenny!*

Something had happened between the two of them. A fight—maybe the two of them, maybe there were others, too. She hoped it had nothing to do with girls. Weren't they still too young for that?

She figured J.J. would tell her about it in his own time. Perhaps, she thought, she should go back in and check on him after all. She walked forward to shut the front gate, blown open by the wind, and saw a couple approaching on foot. They were a little overdressed for Cape May on a Saturday; the man wore a fancy topcoat, and the woman's jacket was lined with fur. She didn't think she had ever seen them before. Besides, the way they were looking at all the houses that they passed showed they weren't from around here.

"Good afternoon," she called as they approached.

They nodded at her pleasantly enough.

"Good afternoon," the woman replied.

Janet couldn't keep herself from asking. "Are you the new people? Taking on the Abbadon?"

"My brother is," the woman replied.

Janet waited for some further explanation, which never came.

"Very nice neighborhood you have here." The man spoke for the first time.

Janet nodded. "The last dozen years or so have turned this place around. Ever since we were declared a national historic site. Made all the difference."

"So you run a place, too?" the woman asked a bit sharply.

Janet waved to the tidy Victorian house behind her. "This is mine. Not as big as the Abbadon, but we run a nice B-and-B."

"And you do well?" the woman continued.

Janet felt as though she was being cross-examined.

"Well, we do well enough. It's close enough to the cities to get business a good part of the year. Midwinter's the only real downtime."

Janet didn't add how long it took to build a reputation, develop a repeat clientele. Mrs. Business could find that out for herself.

"John should do well then," the man said.

"That's who bought the place?" Janet asked.

"John and Karen Dalton," the man replied. "I'm sorry. My name's Ralph. This is my wife, Angela." He offered his hand. His wife looked like she wanted to keep on walking.

She took his hand anyway. "I'm Janet. Pleased to meet you."

Ralph smiled apologetically as his wife began to walk away. "Pleased to meet you. We're meeting her brother for lunch." He waved as he trotted after his wife.

City people. Janet hoped the brother wasn't wound as tight as Mrs. Business. Running this sort of place was stressful enough without adding your own baggage.

But she had been out here long enough. She had to check on her son. And maybe, she hoped, whatever happened between J.J. and his friend might send Kenny away from her son forever.

SEVEN

John couldn't find enough to do with himself. His sister and brother-in-law were due to arrive in less than half an hour, and he wanted to make sure he was ready.

He might have laughed if he wasn't so nervous. He wasn't quite sure what he needed to be ready for. He ran upstairs, strode down the hall, wiping away a bit of dust here, a cobweb there. The hallway and most of the rooms were in good shape. If they showed them around, should he point out what needed to be done?

John stopped pacing and took a deep breath. He wouldn't point out a thing. He didn't want to appear too needy. He still didn't know exactly what he wanted from Angela. Or how much he was willing to give.

Who cared what Angela thought, after all? It was the inn that mattered, the inn that would give them their new lives. He needed to stay positive, for Karen's sake.

Just walking these halls made him feel better, his shoes treading softly over the slightly worn carpet, seeing the nine rooms in the front hall with their doors open, all waiting for their guests, waiting for the inn to come alive again.

He looked around at the faded wallpaper, the paint flaking off the molding, the hardwood floors in need of a new coat of varnish. This was a grand old building. He still couldn't believe it belonged to them. John smiled. The Abbadon Inn would give him strength.

He was ready for Angela and all the family baggage she brought with her. Whatever happened, he wouldn't let them take the inn away.

"John? John?" His wife's voice called to him from somewhere downstairs.

"Karen?" he called back as he started downstairs. "Is something wrong?"

"You could say that!" she shouted back. Her voice was coming from the kitchen. "You just have to see this!"

He walked quickly through the dining room. Karen turned to look at him as he swung open the kitchen door.

"We may have to revise those repair figures. Look at this." She waved at the wall behind her. "It looks as though somebody's been pulling pieces away from the wall."

It took John a moment to recognize the spot. This was the same wall they had talked about with the carpenter the day before. Yesterday, the wall had shown some real damage at its base, but most of the rest had seemed fairly solid. Now the old horsehair plaster had crumbled, almost up to eye level, revealing the gray and weathered wood behind. A pile of white, chalky plaster bits surrounded Karen's feet. He could see why she was so upset. It felt as though the whole house might crumble down around them.

"How could this happen so fast?" Karen asked. "You think somebody was fooling around in the kitchen?"

John walked over to get a closer look at the destruction.

"With this old plaster, who knows? Maybe the damage was worse than it looked on the surface. This might have been the first time somebody's done anything to this wall since the fire. It might have just been waiting for someone to touch it, and then it crumbled." John gently touched the top portion of the wall that still remained. A bit of dust came off on his fingers, but the upper plaster still seemed solid.

Karen continued to stare at the damage. He squeezed her shoulder. "I don't think this is going to come as any surprise to Eddie. My guess is that he was going to have to replace this whole wall anyway."

Karen sighed. "It's a shame it had to happen now. It looks really lousy."

John grinned. "And my sister was expecting House Beautiful?" He guessed he really *was* feeling a little better about things.

Karen glanced at her husband. "Somebody's knocking."

"Already?" Mention somebody's name, John thought, and they just showed up? Didn't that sort of thing happen in fairy tales?

"No," Karen added with a shake of her head. "It's not coming from the front door. It's downstairs."

John turned and walked to the basement door. It was

louder here, a repetitive pounding noise, like somebody forever hammering a single nail. *Bang BANG
Bang BANG.*

"Would somebody want to get in the back way?"
Karen asked with a frown.

"I'd better go down and check."

Bang *BANG bang BANG.* It was rather more insistent than the usual old-inn noise. It didn't sound like
your usual visitor. It could be an animal, he supposed.
Or just about anything. John opened the door.

"Do you want me to go down there with you?" Karen
asked.

He wouldn't mind company. But that was silly. What
could harm him in his own basement?

"What if Angela shows up?" he replied. "You'd better stay up here to answer the door." He smiled as the
banging started up again. "The front door."

Karen nodded. She seemed a bit relieved. "You'd
better take this." She handed him a flashlight from the
kitchen counter.

John flicked the light on and off to make sure it
worked. "I'll call you if I need any help."

Karen nodded. He flipped a switch at the top of the
stairs, illuminating a single sixty-watt bulb that hung
above the floor below. He took the steps down, slowly
and carefully, flashlight in his hand.

Bang BANG Bang BANG.

The first thing John noticed was how cold it was down
here, despite the furnace. He swung the flashlight's
beam around into the corners lost in shadow, looking for
a person, an animal—he didn't know what, really. He
thought he saw movement just inside the crawl space. He

shone the light there again and saw it was only a few brown leaves stirring in the breeze.

Bang BANG Bang BANG.

It came from the far side of the room. The door that led outside was open, slamming over and over again as it was pushed by the wind.

Had someone come in here and left the door open? John stepped onto the dirt floor, looking again into every corner of the room, then shining his light into the crawl space. The narrow area had some junk shoved way in the back, old lawn chairs or something. The way the wooden legs stuck up, they almost looked like bones.

He thought he saw some footprints, kids' sneakers maybe, in the dirt. An old scythe lay on the floor, broken in two.

He thought he heard somebody breathing. He spun around, but it was only the old leaves in the wind.

Kids, then. In and out of here sometime when John and Karen hadn't been around. He'd have to be more careful about locking up the place. He wouldn't want anybody coming down here again and getting hurt. He also didn't want to have any bums take up residence— did they even have bums in Cape May?

He took a final look around. Dirt floor, one lone lightbulb, broken chairs, and who knew what else—this basement was downright primitive. It was also entirely out of public view. This was the last thing they'd get around to fixing. Maybe, once the money started rolling in, he could set up a workshop to do minor repairs. He'd go back upstairs now and lock the door behind him. This was the last place his sister and brother-in-law had to see.

Bang BANG bang. Enough. He pushed the door

closed, and turned the skeleton key that hung from the inside of the lock.

He thought he heard laughter.

He stood completely still, not even breathing, but the noise was gone. Must have come from outside. Probably the same kids who had broken in earlier. Well, from here on in, he would be careful about locking doors.

He took the steps up much more quickly than he had come down, then closed the door in the kitchen and locked it as well. He was glad there was nothing really wrong, but he would be just as glad not to go down there again.

Silly, really. The old basement was just another part of the hotel he would have to get used to.

Ralph Sumner was somewhat out of his element.

He wasn't behind his desk, for one. Well, it was Saturday. He didn't always work on Saturdays. But he seldom, if ever, was away from Manhattan.

He had a very busy life as a part of the investment firm. He had abilities, for which he was well paid. Probably better than he deserved. Ah, now—Angela would call that false modesty. He did have a certain ability to guess the direction of the market; an ability that had only grown with his years of experience. His portfolios were soaring.

Dalton Investments took the lion's share of the credit. He was happy avoiding the spotlight. It didn't hurt that his bonuses were so large he didn't know where to put the money. Of course, Angela was even busier than he was. Sometimes they saw so little of each other, he was surprised that their relationship survived.

But here they were, out together, away from Manhattan. They had spent the morning walking around Cape May, admiring the houses, even talking to some of the locals. To his surprise, Ralph found that he liked it. Today, more than ever, Ralph Sumner considered himself to be a lucky man.

He wondered if they should buy their own place around here. They could easily afford it. Not the size of John's hotel, certainly, just a nice little Victorian cottage within walking distance of the sea.

He didn't think Angela would ever be comfortable too far away from her work. Too many days away from his facts and figures would make Ralph antsy as well. But maybe the occasional weekend, down here in this scenic end of New Jersey, a few hours from New York, would be just far enough.

Angela had finished talking with the next-door neighbor and was strolling down the sidewalk, looking up at all the nooks and crannies of the Abbadon Inn. Ralph glanced at his watch and cleared his throat. "We should knock on the door. We don't want to be late."

It was time for the family meeting.

Angela glanced at him as she tugged on her jacket, patted her hair. Ralph went to straighten his tie, then realized he wasn't wearing one. It felt rather like that moment before they both entered a board meeting. They walked up the front steps together.

Ralph did the honors, rapping sharply on the wood by the central oval of glass.

Karen opened the door almost immediately. She was all smiles.

"So glad to see you," she burbled. "John was just checking on something out back. Won't you come in?"

She was dressed in a simple sweater and skirt—much less formally than Angela. She smiled and nodded and backed away to let them enter—the Dalton family was not big on shows of affection.

They nodded pleasantly, said how glad they were to be here. Basic meeting etiquette, not that different from Manhattan. Ralph waved for his wife to step into the house ahead of him. They did not want to appear too eager.

They still moved swiftly to follow Karen inside. This was what they were most curious about, after all.

Karen waved at a room just to the right of the entry-way. "This will be the reception area—the lobby, I guess." She turned and raised her voice. "John! Your sister is here!"

Ralph thought the room was a nice little welcome to the house. It was in need of some new wallpaper, and it looked a little barren without any furniture, but with the right touches it could be charming.

Karen stood by their side, expectant.

Ralph glanced at his watch. "We've got a lunch reservation for a nice place up the street, in about half an hour."

"Well, John and I can be ready to go in only a minute or two. Do you want a quick tour? It isn't much to look at yet."

"No problem," Ralph said. "We both work at Dalton Investments. You know how good we are at seeing potential."

"Well, this place is dripping with potential," Karen said with a laugh.

It certainly seemed to be dripping with something. It was odd. Every step he took farther into this place, Ralph could feel it more. Maybe it was the light, or a faint musty smell in the air. Ralph had never quite had this sort of impression inside someone's home—or inn, he guessed. The building really felt as if it was from another era; as if, when they had stepped over the threshold, they had stepped back in time. Ralph almost laughed at the absurdity of the thought. It was like one of those TV shows where you take a train and find yourself back in your childhood. The place felt heavy with history—as if the walls hid a hundred years or more of stories.

He shivered.

"Ralph?" Angela asked.

"I got a bit of a chill," he said with a shrug. "Drafts, I guess."

"Well, we have a few of those as well." Karen was laughing a bit too quickly. Ralph supposed her nervousness was quite understandable. "We're hoping curtains and furniture will cut down on the breezes."

"I'm sure they will." His wife spoke at last. He had never seen Angela on such good behavior. Ralph realized he had been making most of the conversation. For a change, he seemed to be leading the way. And Angela was the quiet one, only speaking when she was spoken to. This was doubly odd. It didn't feel right at all.

"Well, we've shown you the front room. There's a small apartment to our left where we'll live, once we fix the place up." She opened a door to her right. "This room was set up to be a bar. We'd need a liquor license, of course, and they're not easy to come by."

The room seemed drearier than the last. Part of the paper in here had been scraped away, as if the last owner had given up on home repairs. The big windows in the front room let in more direct light as well, but the windows here were far smaller, and being only a few feet away from the house next door, didn't allow for any real sunshine.

Ralph realized he was being hypercritical. There was something about this old hotel, something unsettling, more than just relatives nervous to find a common ground. Ralph would often have feelings about stocks, futures, the direction of the market; feelings he had learned to trust. This was the first time he had feelings about his physical surroundings. By walking into this hotel, he had stepped into some new place. There was something here he had never felt before.

Angela and he might still come back to Cape May, but he doubted they would ever stay here. They would find a home of their own. A home with a feeling that Ralph could warm to.

He looked to the others and realized that everyone had stopped talking.

"John!" Karen called again.

"Sorry!" John came rushing into the room from a second door that led toward the back of the house, a flashlight in his hand. He looked down at it as if only now realizing it was there. "Sorry. I was in the cellar. We heard a noise."

"And?" Karen prompted.

John shook his head and grinned. "It was nothing.

The back door was swinging open in the wind. The real estate agent had probably forgotten to lock the door."

"Oh, dear," Angela remarked. "If you're sure that's all it was."

John shrugged. "It might have been kids coming in, looking for mischief. But they can't do much, really. We don't really have anything here yet."

They could say that again. Maybe it was the emptiness of this place that Ralph found oppressive. He still couldn't get over his edgy feeling.

"But I'm forgetting my manners. I'm glad you're here." John stuck out his hand. Ralph shook it. He found the physical contact reassuring, pulling him back into the here and now. What was the matter with him?

"Karen's been giving us a bit of a tour," he said.

"I've only begun really. We were just going to walk through the dining room and take a peek in the kitchen."

Ralph glanced at his watch again. "Not to butt in, but we might want to head out to the restaurant shortly. Our reservation is in twenty minutes."

"It's only up the street." Angela patted him on the shoulder. "Promptness is very important to my Ralph. I still think we have time to see a room or two."

Ralph nodded. Surely he could stay for that long. What was the matter with him? He buttoned the front of his topcoat and followed the others into the next room.

"Well, anyway, this is the dining room," Karen continued. "We're planning to reopen this eventually for dinner, although initially, we'll just be serving breakfast."

"Eggs, baked goods. B-and-B fare," John added.

This was quite a large room, and far brighter, with tall windows on three sides. Yes, this would make a very nice restaurant. He saw it had a separate entrance as well. It reminded Ralph of a grand ballroom, what with all the floor space and the high Victorian ceiling. It was odd how his feelings for the place changed from room to room.

Karen had continued to walk, the others close behind. Ralph hurried to catch up.

"The kitchen has been built off the back here. This is the first thing we need to repair." She pushed open a swinging door and stepped into the room beyond. Angela, then John, walked after her.

Ralph's feet seemed anchored to the floor. He felt the coldness rise into this throat. He didn't want to go into the kitchen at all.

"I think the former owner had a kitchen fire," Karen's voice carried from the other room. "It was the reason they closed the place down.

He peeked through the door, saw the crumbling wall, blackened around the edges.

"It doesn't look that bad," Angela remarked. "That kind of fire could have burned down the whole place." She ran her hand along the blackened plaster. "I wonder if it was an excuse for them to leave. Take the insurance money and run." She laughed. "Oh, well. Their misfortune is your gain."

"I suppose," Karen replied as if she wasn't really listening. "I think our carpenter's going to tackle this first thing next week."

Angela looked back at her husband in the doorway. Was she going to tell him to come in?

"My poor Ralph is getting antsy. He hates to be late."

Let them think that. Right now, he just wanted to be out of here.

"We'll get our coats." They all began to walk toward the dining room. Ralph turned around and led the way back to the lobby.

John and Karen retrieved their coats from where they were piled on the front desk.

"It is a nice old building," Angela offered. She glanced at Ralph.

"I'm sure with a little work, it will have real possibilities," he quickly added, knowing it was expected of him.

Now that he was in the front room of the hotel, he didn't feel so strange. It was something to do with the space, the hollow echo your feet made when they walked from room to room. Maybe he simply hadn't spent enough time in empty buildings. He was sure, once they'd fixed the place up a bit, that the feelings would go away.

"And you haven't even taken a look upstairs," Karen offered. "The rooms are finished on the second floor, and we have some room for expansion on the third. And then there's the attic!"

It sounded as if she was reluctant to have the tour end—as if she wanted to keep them in this place forever.

Ralph forced himself to smile.

"I'm sure we'll have plenty of time to look at everything," Angela added.

Yes, some other time, Ralph thought. Please let it be some other time.

He let John open the door and show them out. Ralph

took a deep breath. The fresh air smelled wonderful. He would relax once he got a little food in him. Karen, he thought, wasn't the only one to get a slight case of nerves.

What else could it be?

EIGHT

Karen found herself alone in the kitchen again. She needed to sit for a while. John had gone upstairs, and it was very quiet. She opened the cupboard that held the box full of envelopes. She stared at the box. She didn't want to open it quite yet.

It hadn't been a bad luncheon. The restaurant had been very quiet, the waiters extremely attentive. The decor was a bit fussier than what Karen might like for their own place. The owners there had a fondness for small, pseudo-classical statues, the kind with missing arms and added fig leaves.

The food was quite good—Northern Italian, according to the menu—she had eaten maybe the best piece of veal she had ever tasted. The salad had been amazingly fresh, considering the time of year. She hadn't even tried the side of pasta—there had simply been too much food.

And of course, Ralph and Angela had insisted on wine. They had brought a couple bottles for the occasion. Neither Karen nor John were heavy drinkers. They'd have the occasional glass at night to relax, maybe more on special occasions. She just wasn't used to drinking during the day. So she sipped at her glass, which Ralph refilled at every opportunity. She felt now that she had drunk more than she had meant to. Her head was still fuzzy, even after that strong cup of coffee she had had at the end of the meal.

But with the wine around, everyone had seemed to relax. Angela and Ralph had appeared willing to work with them. John had even gotten Angela to back down a couple times when she got a bit too aggressive with her suggestions for success in the tourist trade—as if she had any more experience than them! Angela insisted she had no interest in running the Abbadon. At most, she and Ralph would want to use the hotel as a base of temporary operations while they looked for other local investments. They would gladly pay them rent for the use of a room or two.

It had sounded like easy money with no strings attached, but—as she slowly sobered up, Karen realized there had been no real specifics about how much money, or how soon it would come.

Still, Karen had been proud of how well John had fit in. He and Angela had kidded each other about how they acted as kids. Angela, the middle child, a few years older than John, had been the organizer. Little surprise there. Apparently, there was no yearbook or prom that escaped Angela's input. John, the baby of the family, didn't want to do anything but hit the books. Besides a brief flirtation with the math club, he had stayed away from any and all social opportunities. No surprise there, either, Karen supposed.

And yet she could see how the two of them had gotten along as kids. Seeing her younger brother always hitting the books had caused Angela to knuckle down when she got to college. Watching Angela and her never-ending proms had actually given John a few social skills. They had laughed at how they had joined with their older brother, Tip, to deal with their overprotective mother and always-absent father. For the first time, Karen could see how they actually functioned as a family.

The lunch had taken close to three hours. Karen was glad that Ralph had begged off coming back to the hotel to finish the tour. "Plenty of time for that." Angela and Ralph had gone back to their hotel, and John and Karen had walked the two blocks back to the Abbadon.

It was only once they had gotten back inside that Karen realized how tired she was. The wine and the conversation had left her drained. And John, who had drunk somewhat more than she—well, she was too tired to do any planning or start any of the hundred small jobs they could do on their own. She was too tired to even talk.

She had collapsed, but her husband had done quite the opposite. John had seemed happy, until he had gotten back to the hotel. Whenever his family was concerned, he was always Jekyll and Hyde.

As soon as they had stepped back into the lobby, up jumped the family demons. She could see it in the way his face fell, as if the responsibilities of repairing and reopening an old hotel were more than he could bear.

She had asked if he wanted to talk. He had started to snap back but stopped himself, saying he was all talked out. He had muttered something about checking on some problems on the second floor and had taken off up the stairs before Karen could say another word.

She hoped there was some way John could calm his fears. How much easier would it be if they actually could work with his sister?

Since John was off burning manic energy, she had decided to take an inventory of the things that had been left behind in the kitchen. But she couldn't concentrate. And she couldn't hear John upstairs. Surely he should be pacing around or pounding on something.

She decided to go looking for him. She climbed the stairs to the second floor and called his name. It was quiet here, too. She climbed the narrower stairs that led up to the third floor, thinking absently that they would have to put some sort of barrier here to keep the guests from wandering into the unfinished parts of the hotel. It was no longer quite as quiet up here. The cold February breeze rattled the ancient windows. She called John's name again.

"Karen?" His voice was faint but clear. "Wait a minute!"

She heard him coming down the steps at the far end of the hall, his shoes clanging against the circular metal staircase that led to the attic and the cupola above.

He waved a couple pages of yellow notebook paper. "I've been looking at the roof, making some notes. These rooms upstairs could be made into something fancy—guest suites, maybe. With a little work, this place could really be a moneymaker."

She found herself smiling back at him. "Well, that's what we're hoping."

"Hey, if my sister's going to be around here, I have to stay one step ahead of her."

"You want to tell me about it?"

He looked down at his notes. "Maybe in a minute. I want to check out a couple more things. He waved at her as he headed back toward the stairs. "I'll come down in a few minutes. Ten, twenty minutes, tops!"

Well, Karen thought, this day would bring no end of surprises. She expected John would be overwhelmed by his sister—Angela always made Karen feel a bit like that, without the family history—and that his nervous energy would leave him depressed, moping about the upper stories. Instead, he seemed to be making plans.

She wished he would include her in those plans a little earlier on. Maybe that was too much to hope for just yet.

She went back to the kitchen to wait.

The box of letters was there for her.

She would give John his space for now. But he couldn't keep excluding her. They had talked about some of their dreams, running the inn.

They still had to check out the rooms, see which ones were truly ready—or nearly ready—for paying guests. Things would be much easier if they could get some money coming in during the spring. That was what they should be talking about—not some pie-in-the-sky plans for further renovations.

She sat down and opened the box. She had tucked the letter she had read behind the others. She pulled out the next letter in the front.

John made plans, she read letters. She supposed they all had to find solace somewhere.

Karen frowned. This one was different. It was only a single folded page. And once she opened it, she realized the page was mostly blank. Only a couple of lines, written large.

Dear Lucy,

> *I miss you so much!*
> *But then, you always knew what I was thinking.*

> *All my love,*
> *J.*

Her heart sank a bit. That was all? She had been spoiled by the first letter in the box, waiting for each of them to tell their story. The next one, surely, would have more to it. How many more should she read? Right now, she felt like going through the entire box. Well, maybe not the entire box. But she would certainly read another.

She pulled out the next letter in the queue and was relieved to see a much thicker packet than the one before— at least three folded pages. No, four. She unfolded them with care, and smoothed them out on the counter before she began to read.

Dear Lucy,

> *As if we didn't have enough trouble, I think we're getting broken into by some of the local teenagers.*

Karen stopped, looking over to the cellar door. Teenagers. She guessed some problems came back again and again. She turned back to the letter.

Tito has a plan. We've started to repair the place, at least a bit. He wants to use it as a base of operations until he works more deals down here. You remember how the former owners really let it run down. According to the locals, they let some old, crazy guy live in here for years. He wasn't much on fixing things up—or basic hygiene, for that matter. Except for a couple of rooms, most of the second floor looked like nobody had been up there in years. The third floor's half finished. The attic's nothing but junk. The crazy man had lived mostly in the dining room and the kitchen. He had set up a cot in one corner of the big room, and surrounded himself with trash—piles of magazines and newspapers, mostly.

You never saw the place before we cleaned it out. It was like a maze in here, piles of papers stacked six feet high, filling up all but his living space and a couple of narrow passageways, like the old guy was barricading himself against the world.

I think I told you Tito won this place in a poker game. From the way the former owner talked up the Abbadon, Tito thought he was getting a lot more than a broken-down inn. The other guy probably thought he was getting away with something. But after he saw what he'd really gotten, I heard Tito sent someone to break the guy's legs, just as a way to say thank-you.

That's what I heard, anyway. I had just come on the payroll back then, and was keeping a low profile. Silent Jack, they called me then. Can you imagine? Now you can't shut me up.

But what was Tito going to do with the broken-down Abbadon Inn? His first impulse was to tear the old place down. He probably could have done it, too, if he had acted fast. He had already given little, and not so little, gifts to half the guys in local government. So he could have gotten the permits, got enough of the locals to look the other way for a week or two until all that was left of the hotel was a hole in the ground.

Sometimes I wish Tito had gone ahead with that back then, back when he had the chance.

But Tito was always trying to stay three steps ahead of the pack. He was spending all his time up in Trenton, wining and dining the characters who could really bring gambling to the Jersey Shore.

What did he need this little jerk-off inn when he could get a big chunk of beachfront property? All the bigwigs were telling him just what he wanted to hear. A couple of them even wanted to invest. It was only a matter of time before Cape May had its first casino—right on the oceanfront. People are looking for new entertainment today. The World of Tomorrow, like at Disneyland. So he would give them a neon wonderland on the beach; casino, hotel, four-star restaurant, the works— and use the Abbadon lot for something else—valet parking maybe.

Tito, of course, never counted on the bluenoses.

You've seen the Abbadon. It looked like a dump, but you could tell it was a good, solid building. A classic larger Victorian, the locals called it. They had heard the rumors about what Tito wanted to do, and you just didn't tear down a classic larger Victorian.

The bluenoses got to the mayor. Even worse, they got it in the newspaper. The Abbadon Must Be Saved! It looked like Tito was stuck with the place. People were watching now. Even with the bribes, he couldn't do a thing. At least, not right away. He's still working the angles on that.

So one way or another, we had to fix up the place. For a couple days, I was afraid Tito was just going to hand each of the boys a hammer and tell us to get to work.

But the boss is smarter than that. He let it be known he had big plans. He brought in a couple of guys direct from Italy who really knew their stuff. And everything was going fine—two weeks in, and the second floor looked better than it had in years. Once they got the old rooms on the first two floors back into shape, he was going to start them on the shambles of the third floor—maybe even convert the attic into a couple rooms for the help.

Tito gave up the idea of doing anything to the basement. The dirt floor of the full basement would get damp during storms, and somebody told us the crawl space under most of the hotel was built over an underground stream. The locals say that some of the places around here flood on a regular basis. Just what Tito needed to hear.

So the basement was out. We just had to bring the main floor—dining room, sitting rooms, kitchen, back to a bit of its former glory.

Everything was fine until they got to the kitchen. It seemed like a simple job, replacing a couple of the old walls, upgrading some of the appliances to make it a working kitchen. They brought in a big freezer and a state-of-the-art stove. They just had to make some minor repairs, and the kitchen was a go.

That's when things started to go wrong.

Tito was elsewhere of course. Because as far as he was concerned, the place couldn't have a restaurant without a bar.

Now Cape May is one exclusive place. They handle liquor licenses around here like they were the crown jewels. Virtually the only way you get a new license is if some bar owner dies. Now while Tito would not be adverse to such a chain of events, he found an easier way. Somehow, the licensing board saw their way to issuing the Abbadon a "Special License." Whatever that meant. Nobody ever asks Tito to explain. Whatever the licensing board was doing after hours, I assume Tito still has the negatives.

Anyways, I was talking about our problems, for while Tito was setting up the bar, we were losing our kitchen.

Well, we weren't making any progress. Three nights in a row, the workmen would finish off repairing the walls, to find their work slashed and battered the following morning. And each night was worse than the night before—that final night, the walls looked more terrible than they had before the workmen started.

Tito, who knows a thing or two about revenge, wondered if it was the local bluenoses getting back at him. But the destruction was way too wild, too full of anger. You've got to be young to have that much violence in you. Later, you learn to pace yourself, channel your feelings. You know what I do. Guess I shouldn't bring up a sore subject, huh?

Tito was getting pissed. He told Vinnie to spend the night in the kitchen, and he put me and Leon outside the front and back door.

I didn't see a thing all night. Didn't hear anything, either. Leon swore the same thing. It was boring as hell, actually. We would check in with Vinnie every couple hours.

Nothing happened until four A.M. That's when we found Vinnie out cold, a piece of plaster next to his head. But how could anyone get in? Why didn't we hear them?

Tito didn't want to hear our excuses. He was just glad nobody was dead.

Yet.

From here on in, Tito swears there will be at least two people in the kitchen every night.

This kitchen will get fixed one way or another. Tito will see to that. I don't think there's a man or woman in Cape May that will keep him from getting what he wants. I just hope he doesn't wear us all out on his way to getting it.

But enough for now. I'm tired.
I'll write soon.

Love,
Jack

So the kitchen walls had fallen apart before? She wondered if that was responsible for what had just happened to the kitchen now—if there might be some underlying damage. She bet Eddie could tell exactly where the problem came from.

It was funny how the letter mentioned kids. She supposed an inn would always have some of the same problems. She was surprised that vandalism could be so prevalent in a place as nice as this then realized she shouldn't be. There would always be bored teenagers acting out.

It seemed certain things didn't change around Cape May. John would probably laugh if she told him this had all happened before. She looked at the letter one more time, making sure the pages were in their proper order, then folded it up and returned it to the box. She put it in the back right after the one that was barely a letter at all.

At this moment, it was nice to have the letters for herself.

Why didn't she want to show them to John? Maybe she was angrier at her husband than she thought. Maybe she was tired of making peace, of always being the one who brought up the important things, who made sure he stayed centered.

Karen sighed. Somebody had to do these things if

their marriage was going to survive. And she couldn't see John being all that ready to step up to the plate—at least not until his family gave him some room.

She wondered if that would ever happen.

She looked up from where she was staring at the letters. Someone was pounding on the front door.

She closed the box and placed it back in the drawer. She would save the next letter for another day. She stood and walked quickly toward the lobby.

To her surprise, John got there before her. He opened the front door as she was still walking down the hall.

A fortyish woman wearing a baggy raincoat stood in the doorway. Her hair, dyed a not-quite-natural shade of red, was wild and windblown. She breathed heavily, as though she had just been running.

"I'm so sorry to bother you," she said as soon as the door opened. "You're the new people who bought the place?"

"We are," John replied. "We're the Daltons."

"It's such a nuisance." She leaned one hand against the door frame. She seemed a little unsteady on her feet. John asked her if she wanted to come in. She shook her head.

"I'm Phyllis Radcliffe. I live a couple streets away from here. I hate to bother you. I'm looking for my son." She covered her mouth as she coughed. "I understand he was playing around here." She shook her head, as if she was holding back tears. "I haven't seen him since yesterday."

"Yesterday?" John nodded. "It looked like kids had been in the basement—that could have been yesterday. I went down there and found they'd left the back door open. But there was no one down there when I checked, and then I locked the door. I don't think there's any way they could get back in."

"That Kenny. He gets in everywhere. Mostly, he just gets into trouble. He's probably hiding out in some other house, closed down for the winter. Some people do that, you know? Close down for the winter." She closed her eyes for an instant. "When I do catch him, he's going to be in so much trouble. Do you have a pencil?"

John handed her the pen and one of the notebook pages he had been carrying.

"Let me give you my phone number." She leaned the paper against the door frame, wrote "Phyllis" and her number very large, so the few letters and numbers took up most of the page. "If you do see him, give me a call."

"If there's anything else we can do to help . . ." John began.

Phyllis shook her head. "He comes back. He always does." She turned to go. "Sorry to trouble you."

"She's upset," John said as he closed the door.

They both watched her weave down the sidewalk. "She's a bit more than upset," Karen added. "She's had more to drink today than we have."

"Wouldn't she have called the police?" John asked. "Should we?"

"She says her son does this all the time. Maybe the police are tired of her family problems." She hesitated a second before adding, "Maybe the police have threatened to take the boy away."

It certainly sounded like that could be the case. The woman looked like she was just barely holding on.

She wondered for an instant if the boy—Kenny—was even real.

Karen sighed. "I guess they're our neighbors."

"Welcome to Cape May," John agreed. "Is there anything else we can do?"

"I'm absolutely exhausted," Karen confessed. "I don't think I can do anything about—anything."

John grinned. "I'm so glad to hear you say that." He waved at the front door. "What say we go back to the motel and get a fresh start on this in the morning?"

"I have an even better idea," Karen replied as she walked into the lobby to fetch their coats. "Maybe we should just take tomorrow off and get a fresh start on Monday."

Monday. The beginning of a new week. Barring further weather delays, the telephone was finally due to be installed. It would finally give them a link to civilization—not just Cape May, but the rest of the world. And maybe they could make some plans with Eddie and really get the renovations under way. Funny. A small thing like a telephone felt like the first real piece of progress, the first step toward reopening the grand old inn.

"Once we get a phone, we'll call the woman, see if she's found her son," she suggested. "Maybe encourage her to call the police."

John agreed. It sounded like a plan. They stepped out of the Abbadon, and John closed the door behind them. She was glad that he made sure the door was locked. Neither one of them wanted any more uninvited visitors.

As they turned to walk down the street, they saw Phyllis Radcliffe talking to their next door neighbor. Phyllis was talking with a great deal of animation, her hands moving up and down as she made her points.

The neighbor watched all this with her hands folded in front of her, not saying a word. Long-suffering, Karen thought. Like the neighbor was once again listening to the local drunk.

They turned and walked the other way toward their motel. "I just hope Mrs. Radcliffe isn't running away from her real problems."

John shook his head. "Don't I know. Sometimes I think I might run away from my problems, too."

"We're not running away from our problems, mister. Never again."

John looked at her for a moment before answering.

"Yes, ma'am," he said at last.

The phone was ringing. He didn't even care enough to pick it up. His underlings would manage, work would go on. He had other concerns.

Thomas P. Dalton II was not a happy man. Things were not in their proper place. No, it was people, his family, who were not where they should be. It was important for him to know about his family. Without that most basic information, he could not concentrate on the business at hand.

Family. What was left of his family. Maybe that was the biggest problem of all.

One was gone already. Emily. His wife, his jewel, his first great achievement. Yet she never really understood him, never really accepted her place. Why couldn't she have been like other wives?

It had been torture, the last few years. She had almost completely shut him out of her life, separated, living in different homes. She had said he didn't care about her, or about the children. He made sure they would never get a divorce. But she did everything else she could to leave. He had thought she had pushed him away as far as she could, and then he found she could do one better— by dying.

He still couldn't believe Emily was dead.

He was ten years her senior, he should have gone first. And the way she died—a long illness—cancer— but not telling a soul. It was so like her, the way she treated him in those last years. She would always have the last laugh. There was no final meeting, they had had no final words. Just the phone call from her lawyer, informing him that she had passed away.

He had slammed the phone down before her lawyer was done. He hated anything without closure, anything beyond his control. And that will of hers, giving away all that money with no strings—especially to John. Hadn't she learned that their youngest was not to be trusted? She was encouraging the worst in him.

Emily. He almost whispered her name. How much he missed her.

Now that his wife was gone, he wanted to keep the rest of the family even closer. He was a generous man in his way—he would give all three of his children positions of responsibility. The two oldest were wise enough to accept this. John—well, he would accept it eventually.

He felt an emptiness when they were gone. That's what was the matter with him now. He needed them by his side. Well, Tip was still here, working in the corner office opposite his own. But John was AWOL. And it was beginning to look as if Angela was following John's lead.

The phone stopped for a minute, then started ringing all over again.

Angela knew what he wanted before he even said it. She did most of the day-to-day work, made most of the day-to-day decisions, knew all the important clients by name, kept a thousand facts and figures in her head. She was so efficient, he only realized how much she did when she wasn't here.

He stood up and turned away from his desk to look at his view of Manhattan—quite spectacular from the sixty-fifth floor. Clouds hung above the upper stories of some of the surrounding buildings. He wondered if they were going to get another storm.

He was being foolish in blaming his daughter. He had been the one to tell her to go. For Angela, this was a business trip of another sort.

But his family! He still needed all the pieces. It was his legacy. The way his business was run. When he was dead, fine, they could do it a new way.

When he was dead.

Emily was dead.

Her death was too much on his mind.

Maybe he needed to get away. If the company could survive without Angela, then the company could run without a boss for a day or two. That's what he had been aiming for, wasn't it?

He could only push it so far away.

Where was his daughter? The phone lines had gone out the day before, some place along that godforsaken Jersey coastline. An ice storm inland, they claimed, a thousand homes without power or phones. But they must have fixed it by now. He had things she needed to know, things she had to do.

His phone had stopped ringing. His secretary must be handling his calls. It was far too quiet in here.

He flipped the Filofax until he found the number, then called Angela's hotel in Cape May. He could at least leave a message.

The phone rang twice before a mechanical voice came on the line: "All lines are temporarily busy. Please hang up and make your call later."

He slammed down the phone. The lines were still screwed up. Communications were the wave of the future. Angela said that. Everybody said that. Maybe he would invest in some of those new mobile phones. He wondered if they would even work in New Jersey. Would everybody end up carrying those big clunky things around? There would probably be a brand-new set of problems. Would you actually be able to get through to people? Even in storms?

He would have to ask Angela about that, too.

New technology. The wave of the future. He doubted if he would live to see it.

Angela would be trying to reach him, too. If he didn't hear from her in the next few hours, maybe he'd plan a trip down there himself.

He had other people who could hold the fort in Manhattan. He had one important meeting, first thing Monday. But after that? No doubt he would have a couple calls he should return, a few instructions to pass on to Tip, but nothing else that couldn't wait a day or two.

How many days?

Something was eating him up inside. He didn't want to think about death. He had to use every minute.

Emily.

She thought she had had her little victory. But she would not win, even from the other side of the grave.

He always won. He would have Tip, and Angela, and John. And as far as Cape May was concerned, he would charter a plane and see for himself.

He made a couple of notes, then placed a call to his personal assistant.

"Johnson. I need you to get a message through to my daughter. I want you to keep trying—all weekend if necessary."

Thomas P. Dalton II smiled. Now he was getting somewhere. He would be a man of action until the day he died.

NINE

Monday started out bright and sunny. It looked like they were in for a run of good weather for a change. Eddie climbed into his truck, ready for his first real look at the innards of the Abbadon.

The Daltons had called him, just like they said they would. It was John on the phone—he was the man of the house after all. He had called on Sunday afternoon from their motel and said a phone would finally be installed at the inn the next day. John apologized for calling him on a Sunday. Eddie said it was perfectly all right. It was the only time you could find him home.

Eddie had to admit he was still a little disappointed. He wouldn't have minded talking to Karen again.

Eddie sighed at the thought. Karen seemed like she was a nice woman. She was certainly a good-looking woman. She was also somebody else's wife. He didn't want to get into that kind of mess.

But the news was good from the Abbadon Inn. They planned for him to do some of the small fix-ups on the second floor right away, then follow up with a redo of the kitchen and a couple other jobs on the first floor. When the weather got a little better, he'd do the work that was needed on the outside.

Eddie and his cousin were just finishing up another job in Wildwood. He told John they'd come down first thing to take some measurements, then come back to work full-time, probably on Wednesday.

So it was looking like maybe ten grand's worth of work this month, and another twelve or so right around when the hotel would open for some limited business. And Eddie hoped this was only the beginning.

The Daltons hadn't even started talking about the other improvements, like those two bathrooms they wanted to install in the guest rooms at the front of the hotel. And there had been no mention of the third floor and the attic. The Abbadon Inn could keep Eddie and his cousin busy for months, maybe years if they could establish a good working relationship right from the start.

Which was another reason to keep his distance from the wife.

John mentioned that he and Karen were going to paint and paper the place themselves, which meant that Eddie would be seeing a lot of Karen anyway. The Daltons were looking to start advertising the Abbadon in March, and open at least the front hall of the second floor by May, a couple weeks ahead of Memorial Day, which was when vacation season really started around here.

They had a lot of work to do. He thought of Karen, wearing jeans and an old flannel work shirt, hanging wallpaper. He bet she'd look sexy.

It was funny. Karen was the first woman he had found himself attracted to in a long time. Ever since his soon-to-be ex-wife, Deb, left to go upstate, he had sort of considered women off-limits. He hadn't even gone out on a date in over a year. Maybe the pain was starting to go away. Maybe he was starting to wake up to the world around him.

But, hey. It was already February. He just had to wait a little longer. Like the Daltons said, the summer was coming. New people would show up soon. Eddie wasn't so old, or so bad-looking, that he couldn't at least find somebody to take out to the movies once in a while. He would just have to admire Mrs. Dalton from afar while he let the Abbadon Inn secure his financial future.

Whoa! Any more woolgathering, and he'd pass right by his cousin's house. He pulled to the side of the road in front of Stan's Cape Cod cottage and leaned on the horn. Neither he nor Stan lived in Cape May proper. It was a lot more affordable living a few miles inland, up around Clearmont and Dennisville. Eddie lived in the first, Stan in the second; both were only a short drive to the ocean and the real money projects.

"About time!" Stan called as he climbed into the passenger seat of the truck. Eddie glanced at his watch. He was maybe five minutes late.

"So we're looking at a new job?" Stan asked.

Eddie nodded as he pulled back onto the road.

"Big Victorian in Cape May. About a block from that house we finished last week."

"And?" Stan prompted.

"These people are a little short on cash. We may have to be a little quick and dirty on a couple things, then fix them up later."

Stan grunted. Eddie guessed his cousin didn't approve.

"I think you'll like them," Eddie quickly added. "They seem like nice people."

He didn't want to say anything else. He's let his cousin meet them. If Stan learned Eddie had a bit of a crush on a customer, he would never hear the end of it.

"Here. Have a look at this." He gave him his copy of the Dalton's list, with half a dozen items circled. "That's where we start."

"Whoo!" Stan stared at all the items that weren't circled yet. "This will keep us busy!" Eddie could practically see the dollar signs behind Stan's eyes. Sometimes Stan got a little too enthusiastic. That's why Eddie generally did the up-front talking.

"Man, I love these old places," Stan said. "You never know what you're going to find."

"Ain't that the truth," Eddie replied. Sometimes, these places could be a little more challenging than they'd like. He hoped they didn't find anything too odd. They didn't want any headaches.

All they were looking for was steady work.

Why couldn't he remember?

J.J. pulled the covers tight around his neck. It made him feel a little better. He was in his own house, upstairs from his mother and father.

He shivered, even though his parents had the heat

going fill blast. He knew his mother was worried about him getting sick. She had read him bits of *Science and Health* for over an hour before she turned off the light. But J.J. was worried about something else. Something he couldn't quite recall.

It was worse at night. In the darkness there was no place to hide. He could hear it on the wind. It sounded like somebody was whispering his name.

J.J.?

Maybe it was just the tree limbs, rattling against his window. Maybe it was the groan of that old loose gutter at the corner of the house as it banged against the ce-ment foundation. Maybe it was the rustling of all those dead leaves, neglected in the yards of the summer peo-ple, until they blew to cover every yard up and down the street.

J.J. J.J. J.J.

He turned on his radio, tuned it to the local rock sta-tion. Not too loud. Didn't want his dad to complain. Just loud enough to block out the wind, the branches, the gutter, the leaves.

The voices.

When he closed his eyes, he saw the cellar.

It had been two days since he had gotten out of that place. Two days and nights that he had barely slept.

He had woken up in the middle of the night last night, calling for his mother. Crying about the voices.

Not tonight. It was his imagination. The voice wasn't really there. That's what his mother said. His father said J.J. should be a man, and men aren't scared of anything.

He thought he heard them now, despite the radio. He turned it up a bit, listening to some woman singing about everybody getting up to dance, then Michael Jackson telling everyone to "Beat It."

Where are you, J.J.?

The voice was looking for him. No. His mother said it was his imagination. Dreams. He probably had fallen asleep for a second. It was just stupid dreams. He didn't want to worry her. He should be able to handle it. He was almost thirteen.

Why did he have to listen to Kenny in the first place? Why did he have to screw around in that stupid old cellar?

Why did you leave?

The voice tickled the back of his ears. Was he dreaming this again?

You left me, J.J.

It sounded like the person was standing right next to him. Had he left Kenny behind? But it didn't sound like Kenny. No. The voice was older than old. Like dry leaves. Or branches scraping on the window.

Nothing could get to him in his own house, could it?

J.J. tried to remember what happened down in that basement. He had to remember. Kenny had pushed him down there. He remembered that much. The basement was creepy, and Kenny kept swinging things around. J.J. was sure they were going to get caught. He wanted to get out of there. Kenny laughed.

He reached over and turned the radio up loud. Some metal song was on—the kind Kenny usually liked. He tried to lose himself in the screaming guitars.

He closed his eyes.

The basement was waiting for him.

You deserted me.

He sat up, eyes wide. He beat time to the song on the bedside table.

You could have saved me.

"Kenny?" he whispered.

You can save me still.

The voice was loud in his head. As loud as the song.

I need you now. He's coming again, J.J.! Keep him away.

Did he hear screams? Or was it the radio?

J.J. almost jumped when his mother stuck her head into his room.

"Are you okay, J.J.?"

J.J. did his best to smile. "I'm fine. I'm just having a little trouble sleeping."

His mother smiled back. "Well, turn down the radio a little bit. We need to sleep, too."

J.J. nodded and did as he was told. The voice had gone away.

His mother walked across the room, gave him a quick kiss on the forehead. A week ago, if she had done that, he would have made a face.

"I'll leave the door open a crack," she said as she walked from the room. "If you want anything, just call."

He let the radio keep playing, so softly he could no longer make out the words. He could hear his parents arguing out in the hall.

"You're just encouraging the boy, Janet."

"I think something really happened to him, Don. He needs some time to get over it."

"If you say so." His father's tone said he didn't agree at all.

"You know, his friend Kenny has run away."

"Good riddance!"

"His mother's worried sick. I talked to her today."

"She was actually sober enough to talk?"

"Don, you know the woman has problems. It's not for us to judge."

"Well, I'll still be glad if we never see Kenny again."

"What could be in the basement next door?"

His father laughed harshly. "Boys want to get into it just because it's a basement. No big secret there."

"Maybe I should go introduce myself to the new neighbors."

"Is this what this is about? You've been dying to find out about them, haven't you?"

"Well, I'm curious. And this business with Kenny—"

"Well, why don't you take over a welcome basket or something?"

"Do you think they'd let me see the basement?"

"I think if we explained what was going on, they'd be glad to. Maybe we should all go down there together and take a look. If J.J. can see there's nothing down there, maybe it'll end all this nonsense.

"Well, if the nightmares don't go away, I think that's the thing to do."

"Okay, so what say we go to bed and give your son a chance to sleep, too?"

His parents would go look at the basement? J.J. felt a little hope stirring inside. It wouldn't go after his parents.

Maybe they could find what happened to Kenny after all. He closed his eyes tight, wishing for sleep.

J.J.

No one but you, J.J.

You can only help if you come alone.

Something had almost caught him once. And it wanted to bring him back for good.

The eyes were watching him.

He knew it was a dream.

He was walking down the steps to the cellar.

He had had this dream before. He couldn't control himself. And the dream grew longer every time.

He knew he'd see it, but he couldn't turn away. The creature had more than eyes. It smiled, and its sharp teeth glowed through the darkness.

He wanted to wake up.

Come on in! Kenny called.

The teeth opened, and J.J. could see the bright tunnel beyond. J.J. tried to turn around, to run, to cry out. But he kept walking toward the light.

The mouth kept opening, wider, wider still. And J.J. realized that there was something waiting for him.

Waiting deep down inside, deep within the growing cavity, he heard the voice.

It was Kenny.

Only you can help me now.

No! J.J. wanted to scream. I can't help you! You're gone! Gone forever! But he had no voice. His mouth didn't work. Only his feet, bringing him ever closer.

You can come over now. I'm just next door.

Kenny called to him to come join him forever. The mouth loomed above him, the glowing teeth everywhere.

And then the mouth began to close.

Everything was darkness. But he still heard Kenny's final words.

Come and get it!

The next thing he remembered, he was crying like a baby in his mother's arms.

"There, there," she cooed. He looked up and saw his father pacing back and forth in the hall.

"I'm sorry," was all he could think to say. "I'm sorry."

"You had a dream," his mother replied. "A bad dream."

"A dream," he echoed.

"We're going to go over to that house, all of us, and make those dreams go away."

J.J. wished that was so. He wondered if anything would stop the dreams. His mother looked at him, expecting him to say something.

"Okay," he said at last. "Okay. That would be good."

"There. We'll make plans tomorrow. Everything will be fine. You'll see."

Could his parents save him? J.J. hoped it could happen. But he wasn't sure.

Every time he had that dream, it was clearer than the time before.

He only knew one thing.

Kenny was waiting for him.

Come and get it.

TEN

Eddie was pleased when Karen met them at the door. He introduced her to his cousin, watched them as they exchanged pleasantries. She told them John had gone out to the hardware store, but would be back in a minute. Eddie could certainly wait.

Karen had pulled her hair back, but a single dark strand kept falling forward across her eyes. Eddie did his best not to look at it. Stan started asking questions. Karen said she'd give them both a quick tour of the places they'd be working on first. They both agreed. Stan was curious. Eddie was just glad to spend time around Karen.

Stan made the kind of noises that weren't quite words as they marched around—the "hmms" and "ahs" that let Eddie know Stan liked the place a lot. The inn still had a lot of the original detail. That was a bit of a miracle in itself. He had no idea how many owners the place had had, but usually every owner brought his own changes and "improvements" to a place. They'd seen some real horror stories in some of the other houses they had worked in around here. People who had gone fifties and sixties modern, who had taken out the natural wood and replaced it with plastic and Formica. Compared to some of the places they'd seen, it seemed that previous attempts to renovate the Abbadon had left it largely intact. The wood was all still there. It just needed a little polish.

Karen showed them the second floor first, a dozen bedrooms and only a couple of baths. She actually talked about upgrading some of the rooms in the front with private baths—a lot of the old places had been doing that lately—but that would be saved for next winter. Eddie found himself standing close to Karen on more than one occasion. Her hair smelled as though it had just been washed—with a faint hint of flowers. Stan was the one who was all business this morning, reading from the list Eddie had given him, repeating a lot of things Eddie already knew. For now they had to replace a few windows, sand and refinish the floors, and make some basic repairs. Eddie tried hard to look at the building rather than the woman.

They'd followed her downstairs, then. Her jeans had a couple of small tears in them. Eddie looked up at the ceiling, counting the places where the paint was peeling. Karen led them through the lobby, which only needed a bit of paper and paint, and into what she called "a sitting room," a mostly empty space that was still somewhat in shambles.

Eddie nudged Stan and pointed at the hardwood

floor. "This looks like they had a bar in here." Eddie had noticed it his first time through—the way it looked like something, now torn away, had been nailed to the floor across one side of the room. The windows were quite small in here, and the many shelves along one wall looked like they could easily hold a lot of bottles.

"Really?" Karen asked. "This was where the bar actually was?"

"So you knew about that?" Eddie asked. He supposed that was the sort of thing real estate people would tell buyers—anything to make the place more glamorous.

"Well, I think I read about it someplace," Karen replied with the slightest of frowns. "But I wasn't sure where the actual bar might have been."

"Sure, I was in here once," Stan admitted with a grin. "It was pretty ritzy. They called it . . . the Bar at the Abbadon. They had a name for the restaurant, too. Some flower or other." He shrugged when Eddie looked surprised. "Hey, that was right before Sarah and I got married. We were celebrating."

"That would have been back a few years." Eddie explained to Karen. "The Abbadon was pretty successful then. But a little too rich for my blood. Real high end. Top food, top prices."

Karen laughed at that. She had a nice laugh.

"That sounds good to us. Maybe we can do that again."

Karen pointed out the minor repairs that had to be made in the dining room as they wandered on.

Stan swore as they walked into the kitchen and saw the wall. "What could have done this? Some old flaw in the plaster, maybe?"

"It's important we get the kitchen up and running," was Karen's only reply. "We'd like to open the dining room. At least part-time. John's done some cooking. He's got a couple friends who are professional chefs."

"Bring a good chef down here, the sky's the limit," Stan agreed.

But Eddie was still thinking about the bar. "Speaking of money, you know, that bar means this place used to have a liquor license."

"Used to," Stan agreed.

"Yes, we know." Karen said. "We also heard they're hard to get."

"Nobody in Cape May has a liquor license," Stan said.

"Well, there's a few." Eddie tried to be a bit more helpful. "But not too many. Their number's capped according to the year-round population."

"They didn't want the town to become Wildwood," Stan agreed.

"Why?" Karen asked.

Stan nodded sagely. "Have you ever been to Wildwood? Now there's a nightmare."

Eddie grinned. "It's a real, old-fashioned New Jersey boardwalk resort. Lots of bars, lots of cheap motels. Kind of the opposite of Cape May."

"Oh." Karen looked back at Eddie. "What I read said the bar here had some sort of different license. Is there any way we can find out about that?"

"Sure. It'll be in the records at the licensing board. Town Hall, second floor. Either you or your husband can ask to see it."

"I'll look it up, then," Karen said. "John gets flustered. I'm better at dealing with bureaucracy."

The words were out of Eddie's mouth almost before he knew he said them. "I'll take you down to Town Hall if you want. Everybody knows me. It'll make it easier."

Karen looked at him skeptically. "Are you sure?"

"I've got to get the proper building permits anyway. So it isn't even out of my way." He glanced at his watch. "We've got to get over to another job in a few minutes. But I'll be glad to take you if you want to wait until to-morrow."

"Sure." She smiled as she brushed the hair off her face. "I'll let John know. This is awfully nice of you."

"Hey, it's just Eddie being neighborly. Plus, this way we know we've got your work." Stan frowned. "Hey. If Eddie goes to get the licenses, that means he leaves me alone up in Wildwood with the Widow Kapolski."

"That's the job we've got up there. Repairing her summer cottages. She's a character."

"A character with twelve summer cottages."

"Old and rich." Eddie nudged his cousin. "I think she likes Stan."

"I should marry her for her money," Stan agreed. "Do you think my wife would mind?"

Karen laughed at that.

"We really should get going." Eddie checked his watch again. Only a couple minutes had passed. He really didn't want to go anywhere. "I'll drop by here at nine-thirty tomorrow, and we can head on over to Town Hall. If there's a problem with that, give me a call at home."

Karen nodded.

"The sooner we get all the business out of the way, the sooner we can get started on this place. And maybe you can get this place to make you some money." He led his cousin to the kitchen door. "We can let ourselves out this way. Our truck is parked just around the corner."

He heard someone honking a car horn at the front of the house.

"I think that's John. I'll tell him what you said."

She waved as the two of them walked out the door. Eddie wished he could spend his whole life watching her smile.

Angela should have expected this. Her father would ruin everything.

When the phone lines had gone down, Angela had taken it as a sign. She and Ralph had given themselves the weekend off. Even in the middle of winter, there was a different rhythm to a place like Cape May. On Sunday, the two of them had had a nice dinner in the hotel restaurant, and gone up the street and actually caught a Robert Redford flick. It was the kind of thing they never had time for in Manhattan.

They had come back to find that phone service had been restored, and her father had left a message.

He had dictated it to an underling, who in turn had passed it on to a hotel clerk. "Will charter plane first part of week. Tuesday probable. Arrange to pick me up at airport. Details to follow."

Angela swore to herself as soon as they picked up the message. Of course her father had to rush down here. She had not kept him informed of every detail. And, possibly worse, she had let him run his own end of the business in Manhattan.

He was getting lonely. He didn't have his hands on enough people's lives. Thomas P. Dalton II just couldn't keep out of anything. Especially when it came to his children.

She had come to Cape May and let down her guard. Cape May had let her relax. That could be a major error as far as her father was concerned. She always had to be ready for his next move.

The tone of the message was typical. The trip was planned. There would be no discussion. He could be coming any time in the next few days, and they, as usual, were bound to his schedule—a schedule they didn't even know.

She showed the message to her husband. He grimaced.

"Vacation's over, huh?"

Not if she had her way. Maybe there was still some way for her to work this out.

What would happen if she never answered her father again?

Now she was sounding like John.

Well, she would be out of a job for one thing. But she was beginning to appreciate her brother's point of view. She wondered if she and her husband had enough money to do a little independent investing, without her father around?

Except her father would then use all his money and influence to ruin them, just like he had with John. There was no way out of Dalton Investments—no way until the day that Thomas P. Dalton II died.

Angela sighed, crumpling the paper in her hand. The boss was coming to town. She would have to let John know. The thought of that made her very tired.

The phones would all be working by now. She could call them at their motel.

This late on a Sunday? That was cruel. The Abbadon phone was scheduled to be connected tomorrow. She would wait and call tomorrow afternoon at the inn. She would give her brother one more night's peace. But the message would definitely come by phone. She would just as soon not see John's face when she had to deliver news like this.

Ralph put a hand on her shoulder. "Let it wait until morning."

"I was thinking the same thing." She shook her head. "Damn my father! I'm beginning to realize that a little distance can be a good thing."

"You mean, if you aren't under your father's nose, he can't force you to follow orders?"

"You must work for the same company I do." She smiled, barely believing the words had come from her mouth. This was the sort of thing they would never have even dared to talk about in New York.

What was Cape May doing to them?

Angela suspected her life was going to change here, in some fundamental way. Her father was forcing the issue. She wondered if he would like the results, whatever they were.

She actually smiled at the thought. Something was going to give in her family. And it was all thanks to the Abbadon Inn.

John picked up the phone. It was best to get this over with right away.

He had come back from another of the never-ending errands to see a very unhappy Karen.

"Angela called. It's something to do with your father."

So it begins again. As far as John was concerned, it ended here, too. Angela had told him to call her back at her hotel. He dialed the number, asked for her room.

She picked up the phone on the first ring.

John started out hot. "What's this about our father?"

"John. This is as much a surprise to me as it is to you. I got a message from one of his assistants, saying he was flying down here."

John almost asked why. But he already knew.

"To take control of everything?" he said.

"As usual. I didn't want this to happen. I know how much the two of you have been fighting lately."

The thought of those arguments only made John angrier.

"I don't want him here!" John declared. "He doesn't come to the inn!"

"I wouldn't bring him to the Abbadon. Not without your permission."

That surprised him. She'd never asked for his permission before. But maybe owning this inn did give him a little bit of power. John took a deep breath. "When is he coming in?"

"Why would he tell me? I think I'm almost as exasperated at him as you are, John." She sighed. "I made some calls to New York. I'm guessing he'll be coming in tomorrow afternoon."

"And he's coming down to put me in my place?"

"Probably. I don't know really. He talked about filling

me in on some business matters. You know how vague
he can be."

Especially when he didn't want you to know what he
was really planning.

"Keeps us on our toes," John said with a heavy dose
of sarcasm.

"He's the one constant. Never changes."

"So we have to change without him."

"Look," Angela began, then paused a moment before
she continued. "Maybe there's some way we can agree."
There was a pleading edge to her voice. "He just wants
us to see things his way."

His way. "I haven't agreed to anything!"

"Nobody said you had to. Wait a while. Think of what
you want, what you really want from this family. He still
has to charter a plane. New York's been hit harder than
we have here. The storms keep going north of us. Maybe
we can put him off for a day or two. Maybe we can plan
a counter-strategy!"

"I don't want him to set foot in this inn!"

"Well, that's the kicker. You know that's the first
thing he's going to want to do. But maybe there's some
way we can set him up, to catch him off balance." Angela allowed herself a sour laugh. "He's a powerful
man, he's an angry man, he's a ruthless man. But he's an
old man, too. And I think I'm getting a little tired of his
bullying."

Bullying.

John had known his father was a bully since he and
his mother had moved away. But that was the first time
anyone else in his family had used the word. John was
stunned.

"What else can we do?" he asked.

"Use all the time we have to distract him, so that maybe his interests in Cape May can be different than yours. Maybe we can get him to leave the Abbadon Inn alone."

"Is there ever going to be enough time to do that?"

"Hey. We can always pray for another storm." Angela laughed again. "Look. I'll handle this end of it. I'll give you a call when I know just when he'll get to town. In the meantime, go back to work on your hotel."

They exchanged good-byes.

In an odd sort of way, John felt both relieved and defeated.

"That didn't sound so bad," Karen said as he put down the phone.

"It wasn't. I think at least part of Angela really wants to be in our camp. Maybe my father has finally pushed her too far." He shook his head. He still couldn't quite believe it. "But he controls all the money. If she could have kept him at a distance, maybe we could have seen some of it siphoned off our way. But now, the only way we'd see anything is if he felt he controlled the situation."

Karen frowned. "What are you saying?"

"At the very least, he'd want to own the Abbadon. Basically, he's want to do whatever would humiliate me the most."

Karen folded her arms. "Well, if we can't count on family money, then we'll have to find some other way to make this place work."

If only it were that simple. His father would find some other way to destroy them. Bribe inspectors to close down their restaurant. Mount a smear campaign against the property, or against John and Karen themselves. John had seen his father do worse in the course of business, always protected by the shield of his wealth.

"Well, we still have enough money for the basic repairs," Karen offered.

"Let's hope," John replied. "And we can still keep working on the rest of the place. I want to check my measurements on the three rooms we're going to paper upstairs." He grabbed his yellow pad and headed for the stairway.

"Do you want company?"

He paused for a second, then shook his head. "No. It's better if I pace around by myself."

Karen watched her husband leave. She knew they still really couldn't tell the truth to each other. The whole truth.

When John got really stressed, he couldn't connect with anybody. He had to work it out by himself. She didn't know if that would ever change. At least this time he realized he needed the release and could actually tell her about it. That was progress of a sort. They seemed to do a little better with every crisis they faced.

After another dozen or so life- and career-threatening choices, they should have a real marriage.

She tried to kid herself, but it didn't cheer her up. Money was going out faster than either of them had anticipated. They had figured on moving from their motel to the Abbadon as soon as possible, but they couldn't do anything until they had a working kitchen. They were stretching the limits of their repair budget to just get the basic things done to open for business. She supposed she could have gotten other quotes for the work—they always had in New York—but Claire had called Knox Construction "the most reasonable guys in town." And the repair budget hadn't even included the paint and wallpaper John and Karen had bought on their own. It seemed like they were spending an extra couple hundred dollars a day. If they weren't careful, they would have no money to advertise, maybe even no money to live on in the weeks just before the Abbadon's grand opening. They were stretching themselves too thin. She knew it. John knew it. But neither one wanted to say it out loud.

Karen leaned against the wall. She was exhausted again. But she didn't want to just stand there and stare at the walls.

She found herself wandering back to the kitchen and her box of letters. Her free reading, she guessed she'd call it. It took her someplace else, away from money problems and crazy in-laws, a place with problems far more interesting than hers.

She sat on a stool and pulled out the box, carefully opening the next letter.

Only a single sheet again, and this one was odder than any of those she'd read before. It started out with the usual "Dear Lucy." But then—

Two thirds of the page were taken up with the woman's name, written three times in a row.

Lucy, Lucy, Lucy.

Over and over again, her name in three columns, each repeated a dozen times down the page.

The actual letter only took up the bottom third of the page:

> *I somehow feel you're nearer, if I write your name. Sometimes it's like you never left me. Or did I leave you? I suppose it all depends on how you look at it.*
>
> *We both made too many mistakes. I wish we could take back the last one.*
>
> *I wish I could watch you reading this now.*
>
> *Sometimes, when I write your name, I can see you still. I wonder if you see me?*
>
> *I am yours forever.*
>
> *All my love,*
> *Jack.*

Poor Jack. She felt a bit sorry for him now, stuck in this old hotel, going a little stir-crazy without his girl-friend. That's who Karen guessed Lucy was, from the few details in the letters. Maybe wife—but more likely girlfriend.

She stuffed the letter in the back of the box. Well, that was less than satisfying. She had had a very bad day. She decided to look at another one or two of these before John's father stole the inn out from under them.

The next letter was also just a single sheet. This one held a column of lines, like some failed attempt at free verse.

Dear Lucy,

> *I can imagine what you look like while you are*
> *reading this.*
> *I've heard you need money.*
> *I guess we all need money sometime.*
> *I told you about the little bit I set aside.*
> *How upset you were when I first gave you the*
> > *details.*
> *But I know you're not upset now.*
> *I know what I promised you.*
> *It's there when you need it.*
> *I've left it there for you*
> *Underneath the window*
> *In room 32.*
> *Hopefully it will be enough to help.*

> *J.*

What was this? Karen realized she was holding her breath. Jack had left Lucy money? In this hotel? It certainly sounded that way.

Could the money still be hidden, after all these years? This box of letters had stayed safely out of sight for the better part of two decades.

What if the money was still there, too?

Karen stared at the paper in her hands. Her heart was pounding very fast.

Maybe this box contained a treasure map after all.

ELEVEN

Karen ran up the stairs, letter in hand. She felt like a ten-year-old playing pirate, looking for hidden gold.

"Karen, what?" John called from a room on the second floor as she ran by him on her way to the third.

"I've got an idea!" she called back. That's all it was, really—a whim, a hunch, unless she could find the place the letter described.

She slowed down as she approached the third-floor landing. She didn't want to even think how much it would take to fix up these rooms.

They had looked at the third floor and the attic a couple of times before. "Potential," was the word the real estate agent used. "A total disaster" were the words that came to Karen every time she looked at it.

In earlier days, these floors had housed both guest rooms and apartments for the help. Since then, the top

two floors had been used for storage and who knew
what else? She certainly hoped no one had had to live
up here recently. The rooms were a mass of half-
finished projects. It looked like a former owner had had
big plans (far bigger than theirs) but had to stop mid-
project. The inspector had assured them that the outer
walls were solid, the basic architecture still sound.
Somewhere along the line a few new windows had even
been installed.

So the outside was good. The inside looked a little
chaotic. Some former owner had torn down part of a
wall in one place, built the frame for a new wall in another. Someone must have had a master plan. She had no
idea what the final configuration of rooms would have
looked like. It now looked like they were building a
maze.

Maybe whoever did the work was a little crazy.
Wasn't there some mad European royal who spent his
entire life building an endless succession of castles?
Maybe this floor was the same sort of thing—a way to
keep the inn from ever being finished. Always making
something new. Or covering something up.

Nobody knew what to say when they first saw the
third floor, even the inspector. Everybody agreed a lot
could be done with it. Karen and John figured it was a
challenge they would have to take on a few years down
the road.

In the meantime, she had a more immediate problem.
She walked up and down the central hallway, trying to
picture what this place had looked like close to twenty-
five years ago. The exposed and weathered wood made
the rooms look half like a construction project, half like

a war zone. How old was all of this? The work could
have been started by the last owner. The way the dust
had settled on things, it looked like nobody had touched
it for years.

There were more than a dozen doorways here, some
with doors, some without. Even the rooms with doors
had no numbers at all. If Room 32 was in the Abbadon
Inn, it could be anyplace on this floor—anywhere in the
inn really, if they had had an unusual numbering system. She sometimes couldn't find a room number in hotels built in the last few years. How could she guess how
they might have arranged the rooms a hundred years
ago?

She took a deep breath. She shouldn't panic. She
should just figure this out logically. If she was standing
on the second floor, the room numbers would begin to
her right. 21, then 22 and so on. So 32 could be the second door up here.

She pulled the door open. It was a closet, empty except for a very old, very sad-looking mop. She tried the
next door down and saw a mostly empty space with a
half dozen pipe ends sticking up from the floor. It
looked like there had once been a bathroom here that
had been taken apart. Or maybe some prior owner had
begun to build a bathroom and never finished.

This was hopeless. The layout here was completely
different from the floor below. The money might still be
here, and she would never find it.

Karen felt cold air at the back of her neck. A draft
was coming from somewhere. Pushing at her back. It
almost felt like there was an open window up here.

They certainly couldn't have that. It was already

costing them far too much to heat this place. She turned around and felt the current of air with her hand, little wisps of a chill breeze against her skin. It almost felt like fingers trying to intertwine with her own. What an odd thought. She tried to follow the breeze to its source. She felt as though she was letting herself be led across the hall.

She heard her husband calling from downstairs. She stopped in her tracks.

"Just a minute!" she called back.

She frowned. The breeze was gone. She moved her hands up and down to either side, but she couldn't find the cold draft at all. She sighed. A vanishing draft? Just another peculiarity of the old hotel.

John shouted up again. He asked if she was ready to help him paper the lobby.

"Now's as good a time as any," she called back.

She'd leave this foolishness behind. Still, it was nice to have a sense of adventure about the place. This was a bit of a letdown, though.

A part of her had expected to walk down these stairs carrying a suitcase filled with cash. If she kept her spirits up, maybe her disappointment wouldn't show. She had only herself to blame. She had let her imagination run away with her.

She was sure the Abbadon did indeed hide a few secrets, even if they didn't involve money. Some parts of the attic had been closed off for years. Who knew what they would find here if they had enough time to explore?

Karen expected to have a long time to do so. But

enough of treasure hunting. They needed to deal with the repair and reopening of the Abbadon, one step at a time.

Karen and John stood side by side, studying their handiwork. The lobby had been papered. One room down. A couple dozen more to go.

"It looks pretty nice, doesn't it?" she asked.

John pointed along one wall. "There's a couple places where we didn't quite match the pattern."

Karen laughed. "What? And you can see those without your magnifying glass?"

It was the first step toward their vision of the Abbadon. Sometimes those Victorians could go a little wild with their patterns, but as far as Karen was concerned, theirs was tastefully ornate. They had chosen a very understated light green wallpaper with dark green highlights (tiny pinecones, actually). Borders were a complementary reddish brown—the two colors meshed quite nicely. Karen had first seen the combination in a coffee-table book about Rhode Island mansions. Only steal from the very best—that was her motto.

Of course they still had to paint the moldings and do something with the floor. But the wallpaper was a definite sign of progress.

John had done close to three-quarters of the actual labor—he had kept on working while Karen had made coffee, rustled up some lunch, and made a couple phone calls looking for other materials. John had barely paused to take a breath. Bad news from his family always made John work that much harder.

"This is going to be one nice-looking lobby," John admitted at last.

She threw her arms around him and gave him a quick hug. "Sooner or later, it's going to be one nice-looking inn."

They held each other tight for a moment. There hadn't been enough of this lately for Karen's liking.

Both of them looked up at the same time.

Somebody was knocking on the door.

Karen shook her head. "I'll be glad when Eddie installs a working doorbell."

John frowned.

"You don't think that's him, do you?"

From his expression, Karen knew he didn't mean the carpenter.

"After the words you and Angela had this morning?" she replied. "She knows she'd better call first."

"I hope so." John brushed bits of paper off his sweatshirt. "Who else could it be?"

"Doesn't matter!" Karen headed for the door. "We'll just tell them we're not open for business." She looked through the oval window in the door's center.

A middle-aged couple stood on the steps, with a young boy, maybe twelve, standing in front of them. They were all bundled in their winter coats. Had they come to the wrong address? But Karen could see no luggage, although the woman was carrying a large shopping bag.

She opened the door and smiled tentatively. "Can I help you?"

"I hope we're not intruding," the woman said quickly.

"We're Don and Janet Frost," the man added

immediately. "This is our son, J.J. We run the B-and-B next door." He pointed off to his right.

Oh, that nice powder-blue place with pink trim, she thought. She had hoped she could meet the neighbors.

"Small place," the man continued. "Eight guest rooms. Nowhere near as grand as the Abbadon."

She smiled at that. "Well, we're not that grand right now."

The man nodded. "As the Abbadon will be again."

It might have been the polite thing to say, but she liked the sound of it anyway.

"I'm Karen Dalton." She extended her hand. Both husband and wife shook it in turn. "I'm afraid we've just gotten started here. My husband, John, and I have just been putting up some wallpaper."

"Well, we're very pleased to meet you," Janet said.

Karen guessed she couldn't leave her neighbors out on the steps. "Would you like to come in?"

"Well, maybe for a minute. We don't want to intrude."

All three of them stepped into the foyer. The boy seemed to move a little reluctantly, but he was steered inside by the firm hand of his father.

"Have you been in the B-and-B business long?" Karen asked as she stepped back to give them room.

"Close to ten years," Don said.

Even more interesting. Karen realized she was curious about everything around here. "Maybe you can tell us something about the neighborhood. Do you know anything about the history of this place?"

"I don't really know the story behind the last owners," Janet replied with a frown. "They weren't the talkative type. You seem like much nicer folks."

Karen hoped they felt the same way after they met John. And speaking of her husband, where had he gotten himself off to?

"But the Abbadon has been in business for years," Don quickly added. "This is a proven moneymaker. We actually thought about taking it on, having the two properties side by side. Just couldn't get enough capital together."

This was all good news.

"That last couple who was in here . . ." Janet shook her head. "Amazing, the sort of people who think they can run this sort of business."

Karen wasn't sure she wanted to know what "sort" they were referring to. She noticed the Frosts' son was being very quiet, standing between them.

"Oh!" Janet interjected. "I almost forgot. We brought you a little something."

She reached into her bag and pulled out a plate of cookies wrapped in cellophane.

"Janet's special oatmeal raisin recipe," Don explained. "The guests love them."

Karen accepted the plate. "Well, they look wonderful. But, I'm sorry. Where are my manners? Would you like to take off your coats? I'm afraid we don't have much in the way of refreshments—"

"No, no, we don't want to be a bother. We wanted to say hello." Janet looked over at her husband, then down at J.J. "But that's not the only reason we're here. We'd also like to ask you a favor."

Karen felt her heart sink a bit. She hoped the neighbors weren't handing out copies of the *Watchtower* or something.

She heard John come up behind her.

"Sorry," he said as he reached her side. "I was in the other room cleaning up. Did I hear these are our neighbors?"

Karen quickly introduced her husband to the Frosts.

"We're glad somebody's taken over the Abbadon," Don enthused as he shook John's hand. "We look forward to seeing what you can do with it."

Janet looked over at her husband, then at both of the Daltons. "I'm sorry. I started to mention. About this favor?"

Karen nodded. "We'll do it if we can. What do you need?"

"Well, it's about your basement," Janet continued.

It was Karen and John's turn to look at each other.

"I'm afraid our boy—" Don looked down at his son. "Would you like to tell them, J.J.?"

The boy shook his head.

"J.J. and another young man have been in your cellar," Don said for him.

"Oh, so," John said with a frown. "You're the ones who left the back door open."

"I hope that's the worst thing they did," Don said with a frown of his own. "Sometimes I don't know what gets into these kids."

"They must have been down there when we weren't here," John replied. "We certainly didn't hear anything. We've been in and out a lot, I'm afraid."

"We saw the mother of the other boy," Karen added. What was his name—Kenny? Did you hear he was missing?"

"Most likely he ran away. It won't be the first time."

Janet shook her head. "She's been talking to me, too. I don't know what it is about that family."

"It's too bad we can't talk to Kenny," Don added. "He might be able to shed some light on all of this."

Karen was finding this all a little confusing. "I'm sorry. All of what?"

"Something happened that scared the life out of J.J.," his father said.

His mother nodded. "I think it was Kenny's doing."

"My wife doesn't think very highly of Kenny."

"I don't think very highly of their whole family."

"But, whatever scared J.J.," Don continued, "we think it had something to do with when they were playing in your basement. We figured if we could go down in the basement with J.J., maybe it would help."

"Either he'd remember what scared him—" Janet began.

"Or he'd just realize it was just a regular cellar," Don finished the sentence for her.

Karen didn't mention that both she and her husband felt the basement was a little on the creepy side. She looked to John.

"Sure," he said. "Why not?"

"Great." Janet pushed her son forward. "Go on in, honey."

"I don't—" J.J. began.

"J.J.," his father said sternly. "We're going to do this. We can't have you moping around the house forever.

"It will help you, dear," Janet cooed. "Really it will."

The kid looked like he didn't believe a single thing

his parents were saying. Karen wondered if this could get any more awkward.

"Well, why don't you follow me?" her husband asked.

John strode quickly down the hall toward the back of the inn. Don ushered his family immediately after him. Karen took up the rear.

"We've just started working on the place," she said as they moved into the dining room.

"But it's such a large, wonderful space," Janet chirped as they cut across to the kitchen. "You'll have to have us back when you've had some work done."

"I understand you've got Eddie Knox doing some work for you," Don added as he pushed his son forward.

Karen guessed news got around quickly in a small town. "Yes. Claire at the real estate agency recommended him."

"Knox is a good man. He'll do a good job."

"If you need anything else done," Janet said, "we know everybody in town."

Somehow, Karen didn't doubt that for an instant.

"If you need a name, just give us a call," Janet said to Karen. "I'm so glad we've gotten a moment to talk. We met your husband's sister, and we hadn't had a chance to meet you."

Oh, really? That would be just like Angela to be snooping around. Karen looked ahead at the boy. J.J. had done nothing but look at the floor as they walked.

"The basement's right through here," John said as he

pushed through the swinging door into the kitchen. Her husband was moving this whole thing along. He probably felt the sooner this was over, the better.

They gathered in a semicircle around the closed door to the cellar. Everybody was suddenly very quiet.

Don looked to his son. "How do you want to do this, big fella?"

J.J. looked even more frightened than he had before. "I don't know."

Don turned to John. "Did the kids do any damage down there?"

Her husband shrugged. "They might have broken a couple of old tools that had been left behind. Nothing really worth anything. I think the real estate agent must have left the door open. I remember how curious I was as a kid. I'd be surprised if kids *didn't* end up in an open basement."

"Well, that's good at least," Janet said.

"The basement's pretty primitive," John continued. "So long as they didn't hurt the furnace, there's not much damage they could do."

"So J.J.," his father insisted. "What say we have a look."

"What say I lead the way?" John offered.

J.J. nodded soberly, as if he knew this was going to happen one way or another, and he just wanted to get it over with.

"Let me grab this flashlight." John picked the light up from where he had left it on the counter. "It's a little dark down there." He waved to his wife. "We'll be back up in a sec."

Karen was glad she didn't have to go.

* * *

John had to admit, this was one dark basement. Quiet, too. His sneakers made hardly any noise on the packed-dirt floor.

He was glad to have company this time around.

"Whew!" Don exclaimed as he reached the bottom of the stairs. "They probably haven't done anything to this place in the better part of a hundred years. Well, oil furnace rather than coal." He pointed to a metal plate just beyond the furnace. "You can still see the coal chute over there. This is much smaller than our cellar—smaller and older. I can see how this could work on a kid's imagination."

John looked up. J.J. had only made it halfway down the stairs.

"There." J.J. pointed at the crawl space on the far side of the room.

"That's where I think they used to keep the bikes, lawn furniture, that sort of thing," John explained. He flicked on the flashlight, shining it into the narrow space. The light didn't reach very deep, almost as if the darkness had swallowed the flashlight's beam.

"J.J.?" Don asked. "Did you go crawling back in there? There's probably all sorts of junk back there. Rusty nails. Rats, maybe."

Rats? John certainly hoped not. "We haven't heard anything."

J.J. was still pointing. "Kenny," was all he said.

Don picked up the handle of the broken scythe. "Maybe we can poke around back there. See if anything pokes back."

J.J. screamed.

Surprised, John turned to look at the kid. J.J. had stumbled back against the stairs.

He heard a huge crash behind him. Don cried out. John spun around in time to catch a dark shape moving with incredible speed.

The door leading outside slammed open, then rattled closed. It opened slowly once more, pushed by the wind.

"Did you see that?" Don's father called from where he had fallen to the floor.

"I saw something, just a glimpse," John replied. "I was looking up at J.J."

"It was too dark to see him clearly," Don agreed as he scrambled to his feet. "Wish we could have gotten the flashlight on him. Some kind of squatter. Guess your hotel's already had its first guest."

"I guess so," John replied uncertainly. He wasn't sure a bum could move that fast. He wasn't even sure the shadowy form he had glimpsed looked like a person. How could he tell? He hadn't gotten a good look, but in the instant he had seen the figure, it hadn't seemed quite solid—more like a wisp of heavy fog, or a crowd of flying gnats.

He shook his head. He was probably wrong. They were all pretty shaken up.

"Don?" John called. "What's that on your sleeve?"

He shifted the flashlight beam to get a better look. Don glanced down at it. "The creep pushed me down as he ran past."

The markings on the sleeve of his jacket did look like the fingers and palm of a hand, but they were a cold, dead white, as if the handprint had been etched in frost.

Don brushed tentatively at the marking. "Whoa! That's cold! Must be some ice down here."

Bang! Bang! Bang!

The door was once again swinging back and forth in the wind.

"I think J.J. ran back upstairs," his father said. "Maybe this wasn't the best idea. My son was so scared, he probably imagined all sorts of things."

"Yeah," John replied. "But we were down here, too. You could tell him it was just a bum."

"Yeah. Just a bum." Don headed for the stairs. "I think we're done down here."

"Let me lock this door again." And, John thought, this time I'll take the key with me.

"Maybe I should have looked more closely when I was down there," he added as he followed Don back up the stairs.

"Well, this place was more or less abandoned for the better part of a year. People can take advantage of that sort of thing." Don sighed. "It used to be, a place like Cape May, you didn't have to worry about locking your doors. No place is safe anymore."

When they stepped back into the kitchen, J.J. was shivering in his mother's arms, his face buried in her winter coat.

"What happened?" Janet asked.

"When we get home," Don replied curtly. "We'll have to talk to J.J. about what really happened. I think it's time we left."

He pushed the door open to the dining room, and with a single glance back at his family, began marching toward the front door.

"Thank you!" Janet said quickly as she rushed to follow. "Lovely to meet you."

Her husband was already halfway across the dining room, as if he couldn't wait to get out of the inn. His wife half carried, half dragged their son in his wake.

No place is safe anymore, Don had said.

"What did happen down there?" Karen asked.

"I don't know," John admitted. "I don't think any of us know. Someone was down there. It was dark."

"Someone?" Karen prompted.

John shook his head. "It could have been a squatter. It could have been Kenny. J.J. pointed and shouted the other kid's name." He paused, then added, "It could have been something else entirely."

"Something else?"

"I locked the door downstairs and took the key," was the only thing John could think to say. "I'm locking this door, too. Whoever it was, he's not getting back into this place again."

John wished he felt as sure of that as he sounded.

They heard the front door slam.

"At least they left us some cookies," Karen said. "You know, when J.J. ran back up, he looked even worse. Almost like he'd seen a ghost."

"A ghost?" John thought about the frozen white handprint on his neighbor's sleeve. "Makes as much sense as anything."

"That whole visit was pretty strange." She pulled the cellophane from the cookie plate. "Want a cookie?"

"Sure." John grabbed a cookie and took a bite. "Hey, these are pretty good."

"Welcome to the neighborhood," Karen replied.

TWELVE

Eddie knocked on the door at exactly nine-thirty. A carpenter who actually showed up on time? Who could ask for more? Karen answered the door with her coat already on.

Eddie grinned at her. "Well, are you ready for Town Hall?"

"I've had to do business with the City of New York," she replied. "I'm ready for anything."

Eddie stepped back to give Karen room to come down the steps. "Compared to that, I imagine we're downright civilized. Your husband doesn't want to come along? He's welcome to."

"John? No, all government scares him. Besides, he's out again. I think he's discovered he loves hardware stores."

He fell into step next to her as they walked to the

corner. "The male disease. We can spend hours looking at tools." Eddie waved to the far side of the street. "My truck's parked over there."

The two of them hurried across the street. It was another clear and cold day. After the past weekend's storm, February seemed ready to give them a few days of sun. It was the kind of weather that made her want to get things done.

Eddie's truck was a dark blue, without any lettering on the side. Karen guessed Knox Construction did so well by word-of-mouth they didn't need to advertise. He opened the passenger door for her, then went around to climb in behind the steering wheel.

"So how's it going?" he asked as he put the truck in gear.

Karen almost answered him with some vague generality. But she realized she was genuinely curious about Eddie's take on some recent events. She guessed she already considered him her local authority.

"Well, something odd happened yesterday. We met our neighbors . . ." She hesitated, not knowing quite how to explain things.

"And that was odd?"

"Well, maybe. Not that odd. It was the Frosts—they own the B-and-B next door. They brought over cookies. But their son had been fooling around in our basement, and he saw something down there."

"Something?" Eddie prompted as he watched the road. Karen realized she was pausing after each little piece of her story, as if she didn't want to believe it herself.

"My husband went down there with him," she

continued, "and the kid's father. They saw something down there. Or somebody. But the way John described it, it almost sounded like it could be a ghost."

Eddie laughed at that. "Welcome to Cape May. So your husband now believes in ghosts?"

"Well, he mentioned it, and then I think he felt kind of foolish."

"He shouldn't. Ghosts are good for business."

Karen had never expected this answer. She looked at Eddie. "Do you believe in ghosts?"

Eddie laughed at that, too. "In Cape May, everybody believes in ghosts."

He pulled up at a stop sign, then turned left along a street that ran parallel to Beach Street and the Atlantic.

"Yeah, I think ghosts come with the ocean," Eddie explained. "Sea captains dying in horrible wrecks, widows forever waiting for their lost husbands, that sort of thing. I've been in at least a dozen houses that claim a ghost or two."

Karen found that hard to believe. "So these people you talked to want these ghosts around?"

Eddie slowed to let a woman cross the street. "Most of them seem pretty harmless. There are stories about horrible things happening here and there, but they always seem to be a generation or two in the past. You know, 'My aunt told me this true story' sort of thing. Good for scaring kids at campfires.

"But it stands to reason. The Abbadon probably should be haunted. It's big enough. And it's got a history."

A history? What did he mean by that?

But Eddie wasn't done. "Plus, ghosts are good for the tourist trade. Those new places may have a swimming pool or two, but they don't have a single ghost. You always have to play up the unique services, especially when you're running a small guest house. You can swim in the pool at the big hotel, you can get a massage, but can you get a ghostly chill?"

Karen smiled at that.

But speaking of history, Karen realized there was something else she wanted to talk to him about.

"You know those papers you found?" she asked.

"You mean that box in the kitchen?"

She nodded. "They're a bunch of old letters from the early sixties. Love letters. From a man named Jack Cooney to his sweetheart."

Why was she ready to tell an almost complete stranger about this when she hesitated saying anything to John?

Eddie *had* found the letters. And John would probably look at this whole thing in the most negative way possible. Who had time for old letters anyway? She wasn't being fair, she knew. John was trying to pull himself out of that. But his family was trying to drag him back in.

"Love letters?" Eddie grinned. "That's kind of funny. Wonder why someone would want to hide that sort of thing away? Probably a lot more interesting than a box of old receipts or something, though."

"They're kind of sweet in a way," Karen admitted. "I've only read a few of them. And some of them—well, the guy who wrote them was staying at the inn during the winter. I think he was going a little stir-crazy."

"I can understand that. If you don't keep yourself busy, it can get pretty boring here in the off-season."

She looked out the window for a long moment, then turned and started talking about what she really wanted to know.

"One of the letters said there was something else hidden in the hotel."

"Really? Huh. That's even more interesting. Any idea where?"

"Well, that's the problem. They say where this thing was hidden, but that was close to twenty-five years ago. People have made a lot of changes to the hotel since then."

"Well, not that many. Not to the Abbadon." He glanced over at her as he reached another stop sign. "Do you have any idea of where this thing's supposed to be?"

"The third floor. Room thirty-two, actually. Except there is no room thirty-two."

"I've been up there. There's barely a third floor." Eddie laughed again. "You're right. I take it all back. There's probably been a lot of changes. Thank goodness whoever started on the third floor didn't mess too much with the first two, huh?" He shook his head. "There's something different about that inn. I'm not surprised that there might be something hidden there. Short of tearing the place down, I don't know if you'd ever find it."

That's exactly what she had feared. So much for buried treasure.

Eddie turned his truck off the road and into a parking lot. "Here we go." They pulled into the first space past the handicapped sign. "The nice thing about February. You can always find a parking spot."

The drive had taken all of five minutes. Everything in Cape May really was awfully close together.

She and John had passed this large red brick building a couple times before. It looked like it should be a town hall, even before you saw the sign over the double front doors.

Eddie opened his door. "Come on. I bet we can get this all done in twenty minutes."

That would be another nice change from Manhattan. Karen followed him inside.

He led her upstairs, where a short hallway connected two sets of doors, each covered with clouded glass. He turned toward the one that read "License Bureau."

"This is the place."

She followed him into the room. And quite a room it was. It looked like it ran about a third of the length of the town hall, with a wide linoleum floor and a counter that separated the town employees from the average citizen. It had high ceilings and a lot of natural wood. Karen thought the building was probably nearly as old as the Abbadon.

But besides the age, it looked like pretty much any small government building. Karen saw half a dozen signs along the length of the counter, each one identifying a different department. There wasn't much in the way of lines, though. In Manhattan, when you were dealing with driver's licenses, parking permits, even picking up a package, you always seemed to find yourself in a line ten or twenty people deep. Here, there were just a few people talking on either side of the counter, and some of the departments didn't seem busy at all.

And there was one other difference. Everybody in the place seemed to know Eddie. Five people waved hello within a minute of them walking through the door.

Eddie waved back as he steered Karen toward the proper department, a stretch of counter that appeared gloriously empty.

Eddie walked up to the counter and waved for Karen to stand by his side.

"Inez!" he called.

A thin, sixtyish woman, with her gray hair pulled back in a bun and reading glasses attached to a string around her neck, looked up from some papers she was studying at her desk.

"Eddie Knox! What are you coming to bother me about today?" Her voice was sharp, but there was a smile on her face.

"Inez! This is Karen Dalton. She and her husband just bought the Abbadon Inn."

"Well, good for them," she replied as she walked over to the counter. "It was a shame, a nice place like that going empty for so long."

"Karen, this is Inez Butterworth. She knows everything you need to know about Cape May."

"Eddie!" Inez exclaimed, coloring a bit in the cheeks. "He's such a flatterer. I don't know everything. Not by a long shot. But I do know where to look it up."

"Well, there's one thing we were curious about. It seems the hotel used to have a liquor license. We were wondering what happened to it."

Apparently, Eddie was going to do all the talking. Karen just smiled and nodded. Right now, being a spectator was just fine.

"I remember that." Inez scratched at the side of her nose as she thought. "They had a nice bar. And a restaurant, called the Orchid. Elegant place. Just elegant." She turned and walked back to a row of file cabinets. "When would that be? More than couple of years ago. We've only got a set number of licenses here, you know. One falls into disuse, probably gets snapped up by the next folks on the waiting list. Probably been transferred at least three times over by now. Let me look."

She pulled out one file drawer, making small clucking sounds as her fingers danced across the files. She shook her head, closed that drawer, and opened the one immediately below. This time she nodded as she pulled out a file and quickly leafed through it.

"My," she said. And a moment later, "Oh, dear." And shortly after that, "This is quite unusual."

Karen felt a sinking sensation in her stomach. What could be in those files? Was there something the real estate agent hadn't told them about the Abbadon?

Inez walked back to the counter. "Well, I've never heard of this before. It appears that the Abbadon Inn has a special license. Arranged by somebody at the state level, ratified by the town council. It's still valid, so long as you can pay the fees."

"Fees?"

"Yes, some things haven't been paid these last few years. But if you can bring them up to date, you can have a full bar. It's not all that much," she glanced down one page, then flipped to the next. "In all a little over eighteen hundred dollars."

"Eighteen hundred?" Karen asked meekly.

Eddie grinned. "With a liquor license in this town, you'll make that back in no time. Looks like one of the former owners had some clout."

"Restaurant used to have a wonderful wine list, too,"

Inez mused. "You should call it the Orchid again. A lot of people would come back just for old time's sake."

So what she had read in Jack Cooney's letter was true. His boss had arranged for a "special" license. She did her best to look pleased. She and John were stretched to the limit now. Eighteen hundred? It might as well have been eighteen thousand. It looked like they really were going to need Angela's intercession, and her father-in-law's funds. She hoped it wouldn't cost them too dearly.

"This really is good news," she said aloud. "Thank you very much."

"Never saw anything like this before. Highly irregular. Looks perfectly legal, though." Inez continued to frown at the papers in her hands. "It's been grandfathered in." She shook her head. "Nothing surprises me anymore. Cape May's been here since they built the courthouse in 1848. You'd be amazed how many odd little things we've got around here since then."

"So how do we get things moving?" Eddie asked.

"All business today, aren't we?" Inez replied. "I can get Mrs. Dalton to sign some of the forms right now."

Eddie nodded and looked to Karen. "I'll leave you to fill out the paperwork. I've got some paperwork of my own. Building permits and such. Don't worry. You get to sign those, too."

He went over to talk to somebody at a desk at the far side of the room.

Inez watched him walk away. "Isn't that Eddie a nice boy? Why that wife of his would want to leave him—none of my business, I know. But if I were thirty years younger—" She paused to clear her throat. "Well, now, let me get you some papers. And I'll print you up a bill to bring your license up to date. I know you must have a thousand expenses opening up a new inn." She glanced at the calendar. "I'll date it from the first of March. That will give you until April first to pay in full."

"Thank you," Karen said softly, glad, at least, for the extra week.

"I'll be back in just a moment."

Inez went back to talk to a couple of other women at desks in the back of the room.

Eighteen hundred dollars, Karen thought. She could certainly use that treasure now. She glanced at her watch. Eddie's prediction of twenty minutes was far too optimistic. They'd be lucky to get out of here in an hour and twenty. Of course, neither of them had known she was going to get a liquor license. Potential liquor license, she reminded herself. It wouldn't be official until the bills were paid.

Inez made three quick trips back to the counter, a sheaf of papers in her hands each time. Most of them were for Karen's information, to take back to the inn and talk about with John. She did sign a couple of forms verifying her ownership of the Abbadon. Since she co-owned the property with John, some forms would need his signature as well.

Eddie wandered back over a few minutes later.

"Waiting for more papers?"

"Inez says we're almost done."

"Believe her. Inez is the best." He called out to the older woman. "Can I borrow Karen for a moment?"

Inez waved them away. "Five minutes!" She called.

"We'll be right back!" he replied, and then said to Karen, "I've got something that will interest you."

"Plans had to be filed for every building built in Cape May—including the Abbadon," he explained as he led her across the room. He waved to some large papers on the counter before them. "The original drawings—the plans for the Abbadon—are right here. They're dated after the Civil War—I think the inn expanded then."

Karen looked at the two large sheets before them. They were ink sketches on a thick, vellum paper. She realized they must have been produced in the days before blueprints. All the rooms on all three floors were numbered.

"You were looking for room thirty-two?" Eddie pointed at the clearly labeled room number.

Karen realized she was finally getting excited. "Can we take these with us?"

Eddie shook his head. "The originals have to stay here. For ten bucks, though, they'll make you a copy."

"That's very reasonable."

"They'll take a stat photo, reduce it to a more manageable size. It'll take a day or so, unfortunately. They may be reasonable, but they're not fast."

"That would be wonderful."

She looked carefully at the schematics. First floor through attic and cupola—it was all there.

"These might help us do our work, too," Eddie added. "It'll be easier for us to make repairs if we know what's already behind the walls."

Karen quickly made out a check for the copy, then walked across the room to sign the final papers for Inez.

"I'll drop you off at home," Eddie said as soon as she was done. "I've got to get back out to Wildwood and rescue Stan. I'll come back here and pick the copy up for you when its ready. Maybe we can all take a look on Friday."

Take a look at the letters, he meant, and the directions to the treasure. She supposed she would have to tell John by then.

Why did she find the thought so depressing?

John wasn't there when she got back.

Tools and paint cans were piled just inside the door. He had been and gone during her absence. Karen wondered when she was going to see him again.

At least this time he had left her a note, sitting on the counter where they had been leaving their coats.

> *I'm a bit on edge. Running errands is keeping me busy. I've got a couple thoughts on our finances that I need to talk to you about. I should be back by mid-afternoon.*

Poor John. It really sounded like he was running scared. Maybe he thought if he stayed in motion, his father would never find him. She wished John was better able to talk these things out with her. She had thought he was getting a bit better lately, but he was running hot and cold. One day they would really discuss how things were going, and the next he would be the invisible man. They hadn't really found a way to work together. Without being able to talk, how could they work together against John's family? They needed to find a way to make a stand.

Karen wished words came as easy to her husband as

they came to Eddie Knox. She supposed the comparison wasn't really fair. She and Eddie didn't have any life issues or emotional complications to mess up their easygoing conversations. Karen sighed. Right now, she wasn't finding anything very satisfying.

She reread John's short note and wondered what he wasn't saying. She took off her coat. All the energy she had felt this morning at the town hall seemed to have drained from her. Maybe she'd read more of the letters while she waited for her husband's return.

She went back to her stool in the kitchen.

She was beginning to think of it as her stool. And these were her letters. These moments, reading over the contents of this box, were the only moments she had really taken for herself since they had come to the inn.

Well, she had to allow herself some private time. She picked up the next letter and read:

Dear Lucy,

    Things are getting even stranger around here. Now I think Tito believes in ghosts.
    I've written to you about some of the odd stuff that happened in the place. Remember how I told you about that one wall that we fixed three times only to find it falling apart all over again? Tito thought it was kids from town, playing games on the outsiders, but me and the boys had that inn locked up tighter than a drum. Carmine said maybe they knew a different way in.
    Well, maybe. There might be some extra space here and there behind these crazy walls, but I

*don't know if there's enough room for a secret
passage. But then I don't know a lot of things.*

*I do know there are a couple of places in here
that the workmen don't want to go. They complain
of drafts, jump at the slightest noise, make excuses to do anything else. But they're almost done
with everything else. And Tito can be very persua-
sive. Even if he is seeing ghosts, he's not going to
let them mess with his property.*

*But I can see where Tito is coming from. It can
get cold in this place, very, very fast. Probably
has something to do with the high ceilings and the
old wood. Sitting here, listening to the noises in
the middle of the night, a guy can have all kinds
of thoughts.*

*Tito's convinced that something else is playing
games with us—something that's no longer alive.
Living out on the edge of the world like this, guys
can see things—or maybe just think they see things.*

*This town has a whole history of ghosts, you
know? There are rows of houses around here, each
with a ghostly nanny, widow, or spinster aunt, even
the occasional ruined financier, people who often
failed so terribly in life that they apparently needed
to stay around after death to spread their misery.*

Ghosts are funny things. Or so they say.

*I told you that I started to go to the library to
relieve the boredom of the winter, and now it's
gotten to be habit. I've looked up all sorts of
things about Cape May and the New Jersey shore.
I started out with history and geography—with a
couple detours into things like those crabs I told*

you about. Sooner or later, I got around to legends. And ghosts.

According to the books, it seems people are always seeing ghosts on the ocean. The books suggest that ghosts are drawn to the edges of the earth. People were here, by the ocean, first, both the Indians and the colonists who followed them, before they learned the skills and gained the courage to go inland. They all lived along the water. Maybe, the books say, places like this are home to the oldest ghosts of all.

It's amazing how far back the legends go. Supposedly the ghosts were here a long time before anyone even built a house in Cape May. The local Indian tribes had a dozen ways to deal with them, according to one history of the area.

The tribes around here felt the ghosts were hungry, and they did not want their infants to be taken. So they would wrap newborns in the blankets of their fathers to disguise their scent, tie corn husks about their wrists to show they were tied to the earth. They would even cut small holes in their babies' shoes, so when the ghosts tried to lure them away, the babies would say, I cannot travel with you. I have holes in my shoes.

Fascinating stuff. Creepy, too.

Well, the Indians are long gone. But Tito sure doesn't think the ghosts are. He won't stay in this place any more than he has to.

He's starting to talk about tearing the inn down again. Everybody's been trying to argue him out of it, what with all the money he's been

*throwing around to get the inn up and running.
He says that's small change, compared to what
he'll make with the place on the beach. He says it
deserves to be torn down. "Deserves," like it's
some kind of living thing. Tito's getting a little
crazy, and he's making some of the other guys
crazy, too. Uncle Freddy and Sal the Barber are
sticking together all the time, and Gino jumps at
every noise he hears. Vinnie Fishhooks swears
he's not afraid of anything, but that's just Vinnie.
And even Tito's girlfriend, Sheila—who's one levelheaded woman, and much too good for the old
man (It's a shame you never met her. I think the
two of you really would have gotten along.)—even
Sheila's finding excuses not to show up sometimes, though it's probably more Tito's crazy talk
keeping her away than Tito's ghosts.*

*It's crazy, and it's exhausting. There are at least
a dozen people running around here during the day.
But tonight I'm here alone. It's just the inn and me.*

*The windows are rattling again, but I swear
there isn't any wind. I think all Tito's talk is getting
to me. Sometimes the wind in here sounds just a
little bit like voices, whispering just low enough to
hear.*

*Now I'm talking crazy, too. I've got to get some
sleep. I'll leave Tito's ghosts for another letter.*

I hope to see you soon.

*Love,
Jack*

Now he was talking about ghosts?

Well, Eddie hadn't seemed at all surprised by her mention of the supernatural. Maybe everybody in Cape May talked about ghosts all the time. Jack didn't seem to believe in them. But it sounded like his boss was convinced.

Karen shook her head. These letters she was reading seemed to parallel their lives in an odd sort of way, what with fixing up the hotel, learning about break-ins, hearing stories about ghosts. Coincidence, she supposed—that and a certain common ground in fixing up an old inn. She had the odd feeling that, if she read the rest of the letters now, she might be able to look into their future. Would that be a good thing?

It was probably just a silly notion.

The phone rang. Maybe it was John, at last. She looked at her watch. Maybe the two of them could go out and have some lunch, and practice their communication skills.

She answered the phone.

"May I speak to Mr. Dalton, please?" an unfamiliar female voice replied.

"I'm afraid he isn't here. I'm Mrs. Dalton. Can I help you?"

"This is Universal Moving, Mrs. Dalton. We just wanted you to know that you can expect your furniture to arrive around two P.M. tomorrow. Please have someone available to give the movers access to your home."

Furniture? They hadn't talked about the movers. They weren't planning to move anything for at least a week. What had John done?

"But—" she began.

"Thanks for your attention," the voice droned on. "Any questions may be directed to our eight-hundred number. Have a nice day."

The woman's voice was replaced by the click of the receiver and silence.

Karen stared at the phone. What was John doing? Nothing had been done to the rooms they were planning to live in—no painting, no cleaning, nothing.

It appeared they would have a talk very soon. And Karen would be doing most of the talking.

THIRTEEN

Don Frost didn't want to talk about it.

His wife would pull out that damn book and start reading again. She thought *Science and Health* was the answer to everything. And maybe it was, for her. She hadn't gone down in that basement. She hadn't seen what he had seen. She didn't have it touch her.

He pulled back his sleeve to examine his arm in the harsh bathroom light. It didn't look good at all. So what was he going to do?

He didn't want to talk to Janet about this. He didn't want to talk to anybody. He hadn't told the whole truth about what happened, back in the basement of the inn, to another living soul.

It had happened too fast for him to move. He blinked, and the guy was in front of him. Don had felt a cold that was as intense as anything—a jarring, teeth-chattering cold—for just a second—as whoever it was grabbed his arm and tossed him—not pushed, Don's feet had left the ground for a second—but tossed him aside.

He thought he had shouted. He couldn't really remember. But if he had opened his mouth at all, it hadn't been until he had fallen back onto the basement floor.

Who could throw a person out of the way like that?

Whoever it was had been very strong, and whoever it was had left a mark—marks, really—even through the leather jacket Don had been wearing. And the marks weren't going away.

He looked at the dead spots on his skin. That's what they were, small circles on his arm where it looked like the flesh no longer belonged. The skin around each spot was dry, a sickly yellow, and slowly flaking off, crumbling like ancient newsprint. When he poked each spot with a pencil eraser—he couldn't bring himself to use his other hand to touch these things—he had no feeling in the middle of each of the yellow marks. He had found four of them—three on one side of his arm, a slightly bigger one on the other side, like he had been gripped by three fingers and a thumb. He wondered if whoever gripped him had only had four fingers. Looking at the dead skin, he wondered if whoever gripped him was even human.

He had to do something. He had managed to look at his arm three or four times since it had happened, slipping into the bathroom when his wife and son were not around. He thought the skin was flaking more than before, but the dead spots didn't seem to be growing. He didn't think it would get much worse. But it wasn't getting any better.

Don looked at his lined face in the mirror. Even his wife mentioned he was looking tired, and she hardly noticed anything. Right about now he'd like a good, stiff drink, if only Janet would let him keep some liquor in the house. Tomorrow, he would have to sneak out and hit one of those seaside bars. He looked back down at his arm. Hell, tomorrow he'd go out and see a doctor. If Janet found out about that, there would be holy hell to pay.

Oh, well. It had been quiet the last few months around here, ever since his wife had found Christian Science. He was glad she had finally discovered something that worked for her, glad that it had brought some peace to the house. Just so he didn't have to go to church along with her. But Janet's edicts were running the whole household; what was good for her had to be right for Don and J.J. No booze, no doctors, no matter what. At least J.J. hadn't gotten physically hurt in that basement. Don wished he could say the same. Maybe it was time for the family to start fighting again.

Don Frost unrolled and buttoned his sleeve, covering up the problem so he could keep it to himself. Whatever happened tomorrow, he would face the consequences. He looked out the window, over at the Abbadon. He'd been staring at the inn a lot lately, looking, he supposed, for that shadowy figure to try to get back in the basement. He wondered if someone should call the police.

And tell them what, exactly?

He moved away from the window and turned off the bathroom light. He would deal with things tomorrow.

He only knew one thing for sure, for today and every other day. Neither he nor J.J. was ever going to go in that basement again.

Karen stared at her husband. All the anger building up inside her had to go somewhere.

"I just got a call from the moving company. The furniture is on its way." She paused for an instant, as though she expected John might have some rational explanation. "Were you even going to tell me about it?"

"Of course I was. I left you the note." John looked a bit bewildered. She had started in on him as soon as he had walked in the door. He hadn't even had a chance to take off his coat.

"A note? A note that didn't say anything! And after you made your decision!" She waved her hands at the room around her. "We're not ready to have anything delivered. The rooms are a mess!"

"We can work around it, can't we?" If anything, John looked even more upset than Karen. "They would have charged us for another month's storage if we didn't get it out by Friday. And it was cheaper for the moving company to bring it down midweek. I had to do something. We're running out of money, and we don't know if we can get any more!"

But Karen was having none of it. "Even if those things are true, it doesn't matter. You didn't consult me at all. You're acting just like your father!"

That stopped him cold. He stared at her for a long moment before he replied.

"That's the last thing I wanted to do."

She shook her head. "Fear can make you do all sorts of thoughtless things."

He threw up his hands. "We're running out of money. We need to save every penny we can!"

"To stay out of your father's clutches, you mean? I can see how you feel that way. But to go ahead and do something like this without even talking to me? I thought we were in this together!"

"We are!" He turned away from her, as if he might have better luck arguing with the wall. "I wish life didn't get so complicated."

"Well, it does. And we have to do something as simple as talk. Which apparently is impossible for you to conceive of!"

Karen couldn't remember the last time she had been this angry. She was glad the room was mostly bare. Otherwise she would have thrown something.

He turned back around and looked at her for a long moment.

"Can I take off my coat?"

John looked so pitiful, so lost, that the anger half left her. She loved this damned jerk. But she would love him a lot more if he would open up to her.

"Look," she said to him. "We need to get beyond the fear. Only then can we have a chance of success. Not only with this inn, but with us." She paused, then added, "Take off your coat."

He nodded.

"I know. I'm sorry." He pulled off his coat and tossed it on the front desk.

"Well, there's no sending the furniture back," she admitted.

"We'll make do. We always do. Hey, after all that's happened so far, what's one more complication?"

His complication, she wanted to say. There was no excuse for his action. But why did she want to hold on to her anger? What good would it do her to pound this into the ground?

Instead, she asked: "What say we work together on one of the front bedrooms?"

John smiled at that. "I can't think of a better way to spend the day. Get our mind off things, huh?"

Karen didn't think that was going to happen, short of knocking out her husband with a mallet. But she knew they were going to have to stay calm if they were going to survive what was to come.

"Come on," she said. "Help me carry some things upstairs."

The great man arrives.

Except he doesn't.

The words just popped into Angela's mind. She and Ralph were standing inside the small waiting area of the equally small Cape May County airport. It was a sparsely furnished room, divided by a long counter, behind which sat a single man in coveralls, surrounded by electronic equipment; a radio, some sort of radar setup, who knew what else. The public half of the room was no more than a bench and a small table, really, warmed by a single electric heater that wasn't doing much good against the outside chill. They had already been here for more than an hour, waiting for the plane that would bring her father, whenever that happened. Waiting so that Thomas P. Dalton II wouldn't have to waste a moment of his precious time; waiting so the great man could once again be the center of attention.

They had been called by one of her father's assistants, told that he was en route to the airport, and that his plane would be taking off as soon as weather permitted. The actual flight would take less than half an hour, and her father wanted them there when he arrived. So Angela and her husband had driven the short distance to the local airport to await his arrival. And wait they did.

It was odd, Angela thought, that she had never realized until now how much her father wanted to be treated like a king. Oh, she always knew he liked to throw his weight around. No one's needs mattered but his own.

They had always done things that way in Manhattan. But back in the main office, her father's demands had just been another part of her working day, one of those things you dealt with in the city, like standing in line at the bank or hailing a cab in lousy weather. Maybe now that she was out of New York, she could see there were other things to do. Other things besides waiting in an ill-lit, ill-heated shack out on the tip of New Jersey, waiting for a plane that might not even have taken off.

She glanced back at the pile of reading matter on the single table. In time-honored waiting-room tradition, no magazine was less than four months old. Ralph was currently flipping through a *Sports Illustrated* that discussed last summer's baseball prospects. Angela had paged through some of the more general interest magazines, skimmed some old movie and book reviews, and stared uncomprehendingly at some quick-and-easy

Thanksgiving recipes. As far as she was concerned, if the food wasn't on a menu, it wasn't worth eating.

She was losing patience. Sending her on this trip might end up being the biggest mistake her father had ever made. Thomas P. Dalton II might be as demanding as ever, but he was slowing down. He needed her more than she needed him, and when the time was right, a little renegotiation might be in order.

Ralph hummed quietly to himself. Her husband seemed at peace anywhere. Since they had come to Cape May, Angela had realized how much she had taken Ralph for granted, in so many ways. She was doubly glad he was here today.

Ralph would act as a buffer, no matter how demanding her father was, or how annoyed Angela felt deep inside. Her husband was good at keeping things calm. She would try to find a way to keep things simple.

Once the initial meeting was over, Angela imagined she would get back into the rhythm of things. Once she was returned to her father's orbit, she could go on automatic pilot and practically do her job in her sleep.

But, Angela wasn't sure she wanted to do that anymore. Especially where family was concerned.

Maybe it was time her father learned there might be more than one opinion in the family. She would have to find a way to tell him that while he still thought he was giving the orders. Otherwise, he wouldn't even listen.

Angela realized she was thinking about a new type of negotiation, a family negotiation, a deal in which she had an actual emotional stake. And her brother John probably thought the next couple of days were going to be hard.

The lone man behind the counter listened to his headphones, then said something back to the radio. He looked across the room at Angela and Ralph.

"Your plane should be landing in a couple minutes."

Ralph grinned at Angela. He tossed his magazine back on the pile.

"Showtime," she replied.

They both stood and walked over to the window that looked out on the single runway.

A small plane—no more than a four-seater—skimmed above the trees to touch down at the far end. Angela realized she was holding her breath as the plane taxied in their direction. Almost as if she was frightened of something. Certainly not her father. He was the most predictable of men. Nothing he could do would surprise her.

She realized she was a little afraid of her own reaction.

"Please stay in here folks," the man behind the counter called as he put on his coat. "It's regulations."

The man pushed his way through a door on his side of the counter, rushing out onto the runway to meet the plane now taxiing toward them.

Her father descended from the plane by himself. He didn't bring anybody else. Angela and Ralph would take care of everything.

He was wearing the usual black business suit, covered by the usual black overcoat. The dark colors made him look painfully thin—no, he *was* thin. He still moved quickly, his eyes were clear when he looked at you directly, and he still had that full head of white hair, but he was losing weight, for him the first real sign of age.

He walked directly into the waiting room.

"Can't even come out to meet me at the plane, huh?"

were his first words, as soon as he had stepped through the door. "This resort living is making you soft."

One of his typical accusations, putting those around him on the defensive. Not that he would admit it. If Angela challenged him, he would claim he was making a joke.

He glared at both of them, his lined face red with the cold. "So, are we just going to stand around?"

Angela didn't even bother to explain. It never did any good to contradict him.

"We're here now, Dad," she said. "Ready to take you into town."

"I suppose you are."

"I have the car waiting right outside," Ralph piped up. "We can get out of here as soon as we transfer your luggage."

"I didn't bring very much." Her father looked across the room toward the exit to the parking lot, as though he expected the car to drive to him. "Thought I might need to stay for one night. I don't see why we can't get our business out of the way immediately. There's things that need tending to back at the office. I expect you to go back there with me."

So soon? "Are you planning for all three of us to drive back together?" Angela was not looking forward to that trip.

Her father nodded at the airport's sole employee as he deposited a small suitcase just inside the door.

"I might just rehire the plane, have someone else drive the car back later. But we'll worry about that after other things are settled. I need to know what's happening here, get a situation report."

Her father was taking over, as usual. Angela decided she preferred not to be bullied. "I already told you what was happening here. I'm in the middle of negotiations with John."

"Only the middle?" her father snapped back.

"Everything is under control," Ralph interjected.

Angela sighed. "Everything was under control, until you arrived. There's a time and place for everything in negotiations. You know how little John wants to see you. Your presence is an unnecessary complication."

"I realize I was somewhat impulsive," her father admitted. "But I have to see to this myself. I feel the need to do things quickly these days. I want my family to be together."

He waved for Ralph to take his bag. "This shake-up has got me thinking as well. The three of you are all I have left of—well, I'm getting older. I need all of you, in line."

Ralph grabbed the suitcase and headed for the door.

"But that's the very attitude that drove John away in the first place," Angela said as she followed the two men out to the car.

"But we can always bring him back," her father replied. "John's been broken before. We can break him again."

And that's how her father felt about John? Angela realized she was actually feeling sorry for her brother.

"I think he'd burn the place down rather than sell it to you."

Her father didn't even bother to look at her as he replied, "John doesn't have those kind of guts." He waited impatiently as Ralph put his suitcase in the trunk.

"If he's polite, we'll let him manage the place. And maybe a few others down here, too."

Her father was talking about the old John, the John they all knew. But he hadn't spoken to John recently, since John had come to Cape May. She thought her brother was showing surprising strength.

"But we don't go now," Angela insisted. She had to find some way to set this up so that there might be the possibility of compromise.

"I trust your instincts," her father replied. "But we have business waiting for us. I want this done quickly."

You go in there now, she wanted to say, you'll find a wall. Her father had only one reaction to opposition; he wanted to destroy it. He could not bear to lose with anything or anyone.

"You will call John?" her father insisted.

"I will call John. You will wait until I say he's ready."

"Very well. Show me to the hotel. I'll give you a day to smooth things over. After that, we'll ask more directly. If he still refuses, we'll find a way to pressure him into complying."

Angela didn't bother arguing with her father's plan. This, she knew, was her father's idea of compromise.

"Are we going to wait around here all day?"

Ralph unlocked the car doors and opened the front passenger side for her father. Angela would be relegated to the back.

Her father looked out at the farmland as they drove away. "Not much to see here, huh?"

"There will be," Ralph replied calmly, "once we get closer to Cape May." He glanced over at his father-in-law.

"Tell me, Thomas, have you ever considered taking a real vacation?"

"Bloody waste of time," was her father's only reply.

Angela sighed and looked out at the flat winter landscape. For her father, this was his best behavior. In the years she had worked for him, she had brokered hundreds of business deals. Nothing seemed as impossible as what she had to do now.

FOURTEEN

Karen answered the phone. She knew the purpose of the call as soon as she heard Angela's voice.

"He's here," Karen said flatly.

"He's here," Angela replied without too much more enthusiasm. "Though I wonder if even he knows exactly why."

Karen could answer that. "This is one of his power plays."

"It's more complicated than that. This isn't his home turf. And I've decided I can't act as a rubber stamp." She sighed. "I'm trying to find some way to turn this power play into some sort of family powwow."

Karen thought that was extremely unlikely.

"Maybe an armed truce?" she suggested.

"Maybe," Angela replied doubtfully. "I've got him

convinced that today he has to settle in. But he's demanding to see John. What's tomorrow look like?"

"Tomorrow is terrible," Karen replied, thankful she
had an excuse to delay all of this. "We're having some
furniture moved in. And it's the day the workmen
are starting."

"Everything happens at once, huh?" Angela sighed.
"Then I've got to baby-sit my father. I'll get my husband to keep him occupied. Ralph's good at that."

"Until Friday, I hope." Karen said. "You know I've
got to clear this with John."

"And John knows that if he doesn't make some com-
promises, his father will try to destroy the hotel. I'll try
to keep the meeting brief. A walk-through is probably
about as safe as we can get."

Karen had hoped they'd be able to get a few things
fixed around here before they showed it off—especially
to her hypercritical father-in-law. Eddie and Stan hadn't
even started on the place. They'd be in here tomorrow,
but how far could they get in one day? And they would
have to find someplace to pile all the furniture!

"We'll talk," was all Karen could think to say.

"Have John give me a call."

Karen hung up the phone. She knew John would
want to talk directly to his sister. She didn't want to be
in the room when that happened. And when their father
showed up?

She guessed she'd be giving him the tour. Telling
him what needed to be done, and how much it would
còst. Angela and Ralph had barely seen the first floor.
Most of the hotel would be new to them.

And then? Maybe she'd give the old man a bill.

If John's father was going to steal the inn out from under them, she supposed, at least he could pay the construction costs.

Angela woke up early, just as she always did back in Manhattan. When Ralph woke up an hour later, she told him to go ahead and take a shower. She was taking notes. Ralph rolled out of bed and shuffled toward the bathroom, pausing to kiss the top of Angela's head on the way. He could see she was working. He knew when she didn't want to be disturbed.

Angela heard the bathroom door close, then the shower turn on. She quickly went over what she would do with her father.

She had seen some lots, quite near the ocean, either still empty or horribly underutilized. There had been a flood in Cape May, back in the sixties. Some of the town had never really recovered. These lots could be converted into faux Victorians—not the modern monstrosities that sprang up after the flood, buildings that now looked hopelessly trapped in the sixties. No, these buildings could pass for something like the Abbadon, but could be broken down into maybe a dozen condominiums apiece. For the lots closest to the ocean, they might even be able to get away with time-shares. They could probably build them fast, and see maybe two or three times the profit they would get from construction elsewhere in New Jersey.

It was a winning situation. She had made some preliminary calls to check prices and availability, and had Ralph talk with a large construction firm in Philadelphia that they had done some business with before. She was ready for any and all of her father's questions. With luck, this could take up the better part of the morning. She would send Ralph and her father off to scout out some other locations in the early afternoon. She needed time to talk to John. She had a proposal that would keep the Abbadon separate from other company holdings, while giving her brother oversight of the condominiums. He would have to interact with her sometimes—but seldom, if ever, their father.

She hoped there was enough freedom in this idea for John; enough money to be made for her father. It was the best she could do this quickly.

The bathroom door opened. Ralph walked out, wrapped in a towel.

"My turn," she announced. "Oh, and give my father a call. Tell him we'll meet him downstairs for breakfast in half an hour."

"Tell him?" Ralph asked, slightly amused. Back in New York, it was worth your life to tell the old man anything.

"He's on my turf, now. He's going to live by my rules." Her father could smell weakness and indecision from the other side of town. If she was going to make this work, she was going to have to be decisive in everything—breakfast included.

"We're on the clock again," she said as she stood.

Ralph smiled at her. "Hey, I have faith in you."

She paused, looking at her husband. "You always have, haven't you?"

Her life had been so busy these last few years that she had spent most of her time taking Ralph for granted.

Once they were back in Manhattan, would that happen all over again? Angela would have to make some changes, in more than just dealing with her father.

"I'll be out in a minute," she said as she headed for the bathroom. Ralph grinned as she kissed him on the cheek. "I think we're going to take Father on a little tour. Making money in real estate."

This would all be fine, so long as she could get her father to sit still and listen. She thought about Karen's comment, about this, at best, being an armed truce. She really didn't want it to escalate into a war.

Karen looked out the window. The sky was clouding up again. A wall of gray was building up in the west, pushing away the bright blue skies they'd had for the better part of a week. Not that she had had much time to pay attention to weather reports lately.

She hoped it was bright tomorrow. The place looked far better with sunshine streaming through the windows.

Rain or shine, this was going to be one hell of a day at the Abbadon.

John was out again. When wasn't he out? He had dropped her off here in preparation for the arrival of the workmen, promising to come back with some more paint and some sort of breakfast. Knowing the choices out there, Karen saw donuts in her future.

So much for John and her working together. As far as their relationship went, these last few days had seemed to be one step forward, two steps back. Even last night, back at the motel, they had barely said a word to each other. She had ended up watching a movie on TV, one of those woman-in-peril films, with some faded sitcom star playing a recent widow who dated the wrong man— once. (Of course the wrong man was a serial killer. He was *really* wrong.) And the actress spent the entire rest of the film trying to get away from him. As if a single decision could actually change your entire life.

She and John had to make hundreds of decisions, just with this inn. Not to mention decisions about their finances and how to deal with John's family. She guessed those movies were so popular because the heroines could solve their problems, no matter how terrible, in only two hours, minus commercials. The horror of real life was much more complex.

The only thing John and Karen had talked about was family. No surprise there. She had told him Angela had promised to keep their father away until Friday. He had called his sister, and she had said the same thing all over again. Karen didn't think John believed either of them.

Neither one of them had slept all that well. And they had gotten up early. The carpenters were due to arrive a little after seven.

She glanced at her watch—seven fifteen—and heard a knock on the door, as if the carpenters had been waiting for her to check the time.

She walked over and opened the door, and there were Eddie and Stan, toolboxes in hand.

"Morning!" Eddie grinned at her, and she smiled back.

She wasn't prepared for how happy she was to see Eddie. Maybe after John's dour demeanor, it was just nice to see a smiling face. She took a step back inside and told the two to come on in.

"So we're going to take a quick look around," Eddie

began. "We'll probably get started in the kitchen. Pull down that old wall, and part of the floor."

Stan waved and went on ahead, walking toward the back of the house. Karen didn't know what she wanted to say.

"Well, I guess you know your business," is what she settled on. "Whatever you think is best." She wondered if she should ask him about the third floor. With all that was going on, she had almost forgotten about it.

He shook his head, still grinning. "You look a bit frazzled."

She laughed at that. It was odd. That wasn't the sort of thing a workman usually said to an employer, but Eddie was so easygoing, somehow it came out all right. The way John was lately, he wouldn't even notice if she'd grown a second head.

"It's going to be a crazy day," she admitted. "My husband's having our furniture delivered."

"I didn't realize. Do you need us to stay out of your way?"

"Until yesterday, I didn't realize, either. He arranged the delivery without telling me. And his father's in town. John doesn't get along well with his father."

Why was she telling him all this? The smile was gone from Eddie's face.

"Anything you want us to do—" he began.

"What am I saying? I think you can keep on working. We're certainly not going to move any big furniture into the kitchen."

"Well, that's a relief." Eddie's grin was back. "We can work around most anything. Even visits from relatives."

"Well, hopefully we can spare you that."

She realized she should let him get started. She was feeling very scatterbrained.

He waved a rolled-up piece of paper that he held in his left hand. "I brought the copy of the old plans. Would you like to put them somewhere?"

Her heart jumped a bit. He had brought the plans. She glanced back at the stairs.

"Can you spare a minute?"

"To go upstairs and find the spot? I don't think that would take very long."

She really, really wanted the letter to be true. If they had that money, maybe they could tell John's father to go to hell.

"Do you need to talk to your cousin?" she asked.

Eddie laughed at that. "Stan's pretty self-sufficient. And I'm the one who always talks to the customers. I think I can take a minute. Is your husband up there?"

"Out again. I think he wants to stay out until his family leaves Cape May."

"Well, he probably knows his family better than anyone."

She waved for him to follow her. "Come on. I've left the box of letters in the kitchen."

She led him quickly through the house, her steps so much lighter than they had been before. It was sort of like she was Nancy Drew. This might be the last week they could do anything with the Abbadon. She might as well have a little adventure.

Stan was standing at the back of the kitchen as they walked in. He frowned as he measured the wall, listing numbers in a little notebook. He waved as they entered the room.

"Got to go out to the truck." Stan left by the back door.

Karen pulled the box from the cupboard and the letter from its place at the back of the box.

"Here it is." She held it up so Eddie could see it, then began to read it aloud.

" 'Dear Lucy,' "

She glanced at Eddie. "She's the woman who got all the letters."

" 'I can imagine what you look like while you are reading this,' " she continued.

" 'I've heard you need money.

" 'I guess we all need money sometime.

" 'I told you about the little bit I set aside.

" 'How upset you were when I first gave you the details.

" 'But I know you're not upset now.

" 'I know what I promised you.

" 'It's there when you need it.

" 'I've left it there for you

" 'Underneath the window

" 'In room thirty-two.

" 'Hopefully it will be enough to help.' "

She looked at Eddie again.

"What do you think?"

He shrugged. "It does sound like the guy really had a thing for her. I wonder if the money's still there? You know, she could have come and taken it."

That was true. It would have been nice if the two had gotten together. Why did part of her doubt it? Maybe, with all the trouble she and John had been having, she could only think about failed relationships.

"I don't know if she was ever here," Karen said.

"She must have been here. She left her letters."

Why hadn't she thought of that? Maybe Lucy and Jack had gotten together after all. Maybe they still lived someplace around here. She'd have to see if there were any J. Cooneys in the local phone book.

"And John's not even interested in this?" Eddie asked.

"Well, he's got other things on his mind."

Eddie shook his head. "You'd think your husband would want to be in on a treasure hunt."

She didn't tell Eddie that she hadn't mentioned it to John. Or that she hadn't mentioned much of anything to John lately. Was this family thing driving them that far apart?

Probably. John was consumed by his fear and anger with his father. And she was feeling ignored. She had a lot of anger, too, at John and his whole family.

She didn't want to think about that now. She wanted to explore.

She smiled at the contractor. He smiled back.

"You've got the letter. I've got the map. So what say we go and find some treasure?"

"Sounds like a good idea to me." She took a moment to put the box back in the cupboard, but she still held the treasure letter in her hand.

"Shall we go?" she asked.

Eddie let her lead the way back through the house. He followed her up the stairs to the landing of the third floor.

Eddie unrolled the house plans, leaning the heavy paper against the railing of the stairs, and holding them out so Karen could see.

"Let's get ourselves oriented here. If this was the second floor, and the room numbers are the same, then we're looking at the plans this way." He stood and pointed up the hall. "Now, assuming the plans for the third floor are the same, we can orient ourselves."

Eddie grunted in surprise. "You'd never know this from what they've done up here." He traced his index finger along the page. "These rooms were originally much larger." She saw what he meant. The rooms *were* larger on this floor, and arranged in groups of three, with connecting doors. "These must have been the equivalent of luxury suites. Maybe they rented them to families. The Abbadon must have been a class act." He shook his head. "I've lived around here all my life. You'd think I'd know."

He took a couple steps down the hall, comparing the shambles of the third floor with what they had planned on paper.

"But look." He waved at the layout for the second floor, then the third. "There's only half as many rooms up here, and the numbering is totally different. There would be no way to guess which room was which from the floor plan below."

She decided it was nice of him to say that. That way, she didn't feel so stupid.

"And maybe it means the money got lost—even if somebody knew about the letter—and it's still here."

Trust Eddie to put a positive spin even on this disaster of a third floor.

"So where would it be?" she asked.

"Well, let's figure out the old layout." He started

looking around the floor from where he stood by the staircase, then back at the plans. He pointed to the right corner. "So thirty would be this way?"

He looked at a frame someone had begun in the middle of the hall, as if they had planned to wall off part of the corridor.

"What have they done to this floor? It's like somebody wanted to tear this whole place down and start from scratch."

Karen tended to agree. This floor made no sense at all.

"A lot of things people do to their homes don't make any sense," Eddie continued, as if he had read her mind. "But this floor takes the no-sense prize." He looked back at the plans again. "That means thirty-one would be over here." He pointed down toward the far end of the hall. He pivoted to face the other direction. "And thirty-two would be all the way over on the other side of the hall."

It was opposite the rooms she was looking at the other day, the direction in which she had felt the draft. She remembered the sensation she had, like fingers of air grabbing at her hand.

Karen thought how she had felt, just for an instant, like something else was up here with her. She thought it was her imagination and all this talk of ghosts.

What if the ghost was real, and it was up here? What if it was trying to tell her something? The more time she spent in this place, the easier it was for her to believe that sort of thing.

She felt no draft now. Did the ghost want to talk only to her?

Why would that be? She half wanted to mention the

thought to Eddie. But she had said enough—maybe too much—to him already.

Ghosts? She was being foolish.

She couldn't tell John about the letters. She couldn't tell Eddie about the ghost. She wasn't quite sure what she wanted, from anybody.

"Well, what are we waiting for?" Eddie called to her. "Let's walk into room thirty-two."

This time, Eddie led the way, past another half-built wall, through a doorway that no longer had a door. She followed him, stopping beside him in the middle of the room—a space far larger than those on the other side of the hall.

"See these marks on the plans?" He pointed to some hatch marks along one wall of the drawing.

"What does that mean?"

"There would have been two windows here. They took one of them out. Heaven knows why."

Karen wondered if the crazy remodeling that had taken over the rest of the floor hadn't quite reached this far.

"So according to the note here, the money would be under the window." He knelt down by the window that was still in place, feeling around on the floor and along the baseboard. He looked back up at Karen. "This all looks pretty solid to me."

"Maybe they found the money after they started this renovation," she suggested. Maybe, she thought, that was why they stopped.

"If that's what you want to call this. Or maybe they renovated right over it." He looked at the plans again. "One more window to go."

Karen felt her eyes drawn to a board that didn't seem to quite match the others. It was a slightly lighter color, and had a bit more space at the far end between it and the next part of the floor. She pointed down at the space.

"How about here?"

Eddie moved over to give it a try.

"It's loose. I can't quite get a grip on it." He pulled a screwdriver from his belt.

The floorboard came right up.

She saw an old tan envelope underneath, not much different in color from the floorboards to either side.

"Ms. Karen, I think you might just lead a charmed life." Eddie stood and smiled. "I'll let you have the honor of picking it up. Somehow, I feel it's meant for you."

He stepped back, and she took her turn kneeling by the hiding place. She tried to keep her hand from shaking as she pulled the envelope from its hiding space.

A few words were written just above the clasp. She recognized Jack's precise hand.

Don't worry. None of this can be traced.
J.

She opened the envelope quickly. It was stuffed with hundred-dollar bills.

"Eddie! Look at this."

The bills were bundled in groups of ten, a thousand dollars per bundle. Karen counted seventeen of them.

It added up to seventeen thousand dollars.

"How much?" Eddie asked.

She told him, hugging Eddie tight on the spur of the

moment. He hugged her back. They held onto each other for a long moment.

"Sorry," Eddie said as he let go. His cheeks were a little red. "A little overcome by the moment there."

She grinned at him. She felt like a kid.

"I wish John could be that spontaneous."

She held out the money.

"You should get some of this."

He grinned back at her.

"That's very generous, but that's yours. Hey, use part of it to put in one of those bathrooms. We'll get it one way or another."

They stood there for a second in silence, neither one quite looking at the other, but neither one making the first move to leave.

"Well, you should probably celebrate," Eddie said at last. "You and John, I mean." He laughed. "You'll have to tell me his reaction."

She looked at the money in her hands. She would have to come clean about the letters to John.

Seventeen thousand dollars.

It wasn't all the money in the world. But it could keep them afloat until they could get the inn operational. And they could proceed with a couple of the more complicated repairs.

It might mean their real independence.

She thought about what Eddie said. What did he mean, this was meant for her?

She thought again of the ghostly fingers.

Maybe, if there was a ghost or two in the Abbadon Inn, they wanted them to stay.

She looked at the envelope, stuffed with cash.

"This is impossible."

"Impossible or not, it's here," Eddie replied. "I should probably get back to work. I won't tell Stan until after you tell your husband."

"I just don't know what to think," she admitted.

"Look at it this way," Eddie said as he headed for the stairs. "Your hotel has already turned a profit."

Karen waited for a minute, then walked down the stairs herself. She felt as though she was walking through a dream. How could all the owners, over nearly twenty-five years, not find either of these—the box of letters, and now this, the envelope full of hundred-dollar bills?

How would she explain it to John? Why didn't she want him to see the box?

Perhaps she would show him this letter, but none of the others. It was like, in the middle of all this madness, she really needed one secret, one thing she could call her own.

When she reached the bottom of the stairs, she saw the front door was wide open. A man walked in carrying an overstuffed chair. She could hear four or five others, moving through the rooms that would be their apartment.

The old inn was hopping. The movers were here.

FIFTEEN

"Karen! There you are!

"The movers got here five minutes ago," John continued before Karen could say a thing. "Right after I did. Oh, if you want one, there's donuts in the kitchen. I told Stan and Eddie to help themselves. I got some coffee, too.

"I've already told the movers what to do. We'll set up the bed and the bureaus, put the kitchen stuff in our kitchenette. The stuff we need to get to right away. I'm going to pile everything else in the big room."

The one that was going to be their living area. It probably wouldn't happen now for a long time.

If ever, a little voice in her head said.

"It's good we thought to mark all the boxes," he started in again. "I've managed to get—"

"John!" Karen held a hand in front of his face. "Slow down a minute!"

She had their redemption in this envelope.

"I need to talk to you."

She started to undo the clasp.

"In a little while," John replied, already moving away. "I want to make sure the movers know where everything is going." John rushed off down the hall. "This will work out! You'll see!"

She waved the envelope in the air. John was already gone.

Phyllis saw her chance.

The new people who ran the Abbadon would never let her in. She had seen them talking to Don and Janet Frost. The Frosts used to be her friends. Not anymore. She knew they would say terrible things about her to anyone they met.

Holier-than-thou Janet wouldn't talk to her anymore, just because Phyllis drank. Oh, she would exchange a word or two. She actually sounded sorry when Kenny went missing, at least for a minute, before she excused herself to do something important. Bitch! What could be more important than a missing child?

Kenny had been in the basement of the inn. That was the last place anyone had seen him. But if she went to knock at the door, they'd turn her away. They always turned her away. Poor, crazy Phyllis. Can't even hold a job. It was a wonder they didn't take her son away.

Well, that wasn't going to happen—ever. She and

Kenny would be together forever. She just had to find him again.

She had to get in that basement. She knew Kenny better than anyone. Maybe he was hurt down there. Maybe he had left some sign of where he was really hiding. She was his mother. She would see things everybody else would miss.

She had tried the outside basement door, in the middle of the night when no one would see her. It was locked, the heavy wooden frame too strong to break through. Had she heard something on the other side? Something scratching, maybe a faint cry? She had to find another way in.

So she parked down the street, waiting for the right time. When the Frosts weren't working in their yard. Don wouldn't talk to her since that night four years ago, and she had no idea why. Maybe they had slept together. Phyllis had had so many nights she couldn't remember. And Janet and her religion. She would turn her whole family against Phyllis. She'd turn the whole town against her!

Damn this town anyway! They wouldn't let her have anything. She had as many rights as the next person!

They weren't going to take away her boy. She'd go and find out where he went. Snatch him back if they were hiding him. She just had to wait for the right time.

Thursday morning, the carpenters had shown up. Phyllis knew them by sight. They did a lot of work around the neighborhood, but she didn't know their names. Neither one of them went to the bars up in Wildwood. She was hoping they would have to use the basement and leave the door open. But they disappeared inside, and, except for a single trip one of them took to the truck, she didn't see them again.

An hour or two passed. Phyllis had trouble keeping track of time. Then the movers showed up, half a dozen guys with a truck that took up half the street, leaving the front door wide open, walking in and out of the hotel, over and over.

It was like a circus in there. Who would notice one more person slipping in, running down to the basement from the door inside?

Phyllis combed her hair in the rearview mirror. She hoped she looked presentable. She should have changed her clothes. She should have washed her hair. At least the Frosts were nowhere to be seen, to look down at her, to keep her from finding her son.

She'd do it now. She had to do it, before Kenny was lost to her forever.

She got out of her car and walked, as quickly and steadily as she could, toward the front door of the Abbadon.

Karen had had just about enough of this. She grabbed her husband's wrist as he once again hurried past.

"John. You are sitting down. Now."

"What? Oh, I guess so," he replied without much enthusiasm. "I think everything's in the right place. They're getting it done fast, too."

Karen had also been impressed with the way the men carted in two and three boxes at a time. She'd bet they'd be done with this end of the job in less than an hour.

John looked up and down the hallway. "Where am I sitting?"

Karen looked around. The entire first floor was a high-traffic area. "How about the stairs?" she suggested. "What say we get a little bit out of the way and go up closer to the second floor? I have to show you something." She didn't want to be flashing large wads of cash in front of complete strangers.

"Something?" John smiled tentatively as he sat down at the top of the stairs.

She sat on the landing next to him. "The house's special gift, I guess." She held the envelope in her hand. How could she explain?

"I found something. Well, it started with a box of letters that I found in the kitchen." For some reason, she decided to leave Eddie out of that part of the story. "Most of the letters are nothing. I kept meaning to show them to you. But then I kept getting mad at you, I guess."

"Mad? Well, I have been running around a lot. I haven't been around here that much lately, have I?" He said the words slowly, as if he was just realizing the obvious. He glanced back at Karen. "But these letters?"

"I didn't think they were very important. They were just old personal correspondence. But there was one letter that said someone had hidden something in the house. I took a look but couldn't find it. I figured whatever it was was long gone. But then, when we went down to Town Hall, Eddie came up with the original plans of the inn."

John looked at her as if he didn't understand a word she was saying.

"Oh, none of that's important! This is what's important."

She opened the envelope and thrust it in his face.

"Look in there."

"Money. You found money." He pulled out a couple packs of hundred-dollar bills. "You found this in the house? You couldn't have found this in the house."

"Well, it wasn't easy," Karen admitted. "It was up on the third floor. Eddie had to figure out where the room was."

"The contractor?" John frowned. "Does he want part of this?"

"No. He says we can just pay him to fix up a couple extra rooms."

He kept staring at the envelope full of cash. "You talked to the contractor about this, but you didn't talk to me?"

"When were you around?" she shot back. "Eddie and I were making conversation on the way to Town Hall. Remember Town Hall? I went there so you wouldn't have to."

"Yeah, and found we had a liquor license. This is all great news. Maybe I'm just tired." He stared at the money again. "Shouldn't we take this to the police?"

Karen shook her head. "This money comes from twenty-five years ago. Anybody who wanted it would have found it by now. Look at the date on the note."

He read Jack's note below the clasp. "Can't be traced? What is this, mob money?"

"Probably," Karen replied. "I think this inn has a colorful past."

John shook his head. "How much is in here?"

"Seventeen grand." She expected John to be happier. "Don't you think this can get us through?"

"I don't think anything's going to get us through," he replied flatly.

"You don't see this as a sign?" Karen had finally had enough of her depressed and depressing husband. "You have to stand up to your family, damn it! Especially your father! We don't need his money! We'll find a way."

"You don't understand. My father ruins everything. That's what he does. That's what makes him happy. It's more than just keeping us under his thumb."

But the words kept spilling out of Karen. "Oh, I understand, all right. You look forward to your father stepping in. That way, you don't have to take responsibility for anything. You can be a failure your entire life! Your father's failure!"

She expected John to get really mad at her then. Maybe she was even looking forward to it. But John only stared for a long moment.

"You're right. We have to ignore my father. He's not going to have the same influence down here he has back in the city. And if we have to depend on found money— hey, why not?"

He allowed himself the slightest of smiles. "Should we put this in the bank?

"Maybe it's time I got a cookie jar." Karen shrugged. "Hey, Eddie wouldn't mind being paid in cash."

John looked at her a long time before he replied.

"You keep talking about Eddie, don't you?"

"What do you mean by that?"

"It's probably nothing. I was just remembering Jeff Lane."

It was Karen's turn to stare at her husband. "You knew?" It had been the biggest mistake of her life. It was four years ago, right after John's second big-business venture had gone bust. With his family's help, of course. John had had to go back to work for his father, and he had withdrawn from her, far worse than now. Without quite knowing what she was doing, Karen had gone out looking for human contact and ended up in another man's bed.

"Hey, it was hard not to know," John replied. "The way you two acted at the Christmas party, the way you disappeared after New Year's. I may be neurotic, I may be clueless, but I'm not stupid."

"Oh, God, I'm so sorry. I should have told you a long time ago. It was so stupid. It didn't last. As soon as it started, I realized how wrong it was."

John studied the back of his hands for a moment before he replied. "We've talked about this before, if not quite so honestly. New York didn't end up being very good for either of us." He looked up at Karen. "Maybe, if we can get everything out in the open, we really can get a fresh start."

"Okay," she replied. "So where do we start?"

"I think we've already started. Plus, I need you to talk to me before you run off with anybody else."

Was that a joke? Karen didn't know whether to laugh or to throw something at him.

"Okay," she said instead. "From this moment forward, we're talking." She hoped he really meant it this time.

John gave her back the envelope. "The money. It's a good thing. I think it will help. But I can't sit here any more. We'll talk after everybody leaves."

He stood up to go downstairs but glanced back up at Karen.

"Did you see that?"

"What?"

"Some woman with red hair just walked back to the kitchen."

"You didn't recognize her?"

John shook his head. "I barely got a glimpse of her. Maybe it's some friend of the contractors. Isn't one of them married?"

A woman, coming to see Stan and Eddie. A part of Karen didn't like that. Why would it depress Karen to think that Eddie had a girlfriend? Maybe John was right. She was looking elsewhere for affection, keeping her options open. Just like that terrible time with Jeff Lane.

"Maybe we should both go back downstairs," she said to her husband. She wasn't ready to have strangers wandering around the inn just yet. Red hair? Didn't that woman whose son was missing have red hair?

"I've got to get back anyway. I think the guys are almost done. I've got to tip the movers."

Karen waved the envelope. "I've got the cash."

"No!" John replied with surprising vehemence. More softly, he added, "I've already got the cash for it. It's a business expense."

Almost everything was a business expense at this point. Did it matter if you saved money on your taxes if you had no money in the first place?

"We'll figure everything out," he called out as he started to leave. "Really."

She watched him run down the steps and disappear around the corner.

Karen stood up. She would need to find a place to put the cash. She hoped the money would help them in the end.

Phyllis was home free.

A couple of the movers had passed her in the hall and nodded pleasantly. Someone had seen her from the top of the stairs but hadn't said a word. She had kept on moving through the inn, opening doors, looking for the basement. She'd passed at last through the huge dining room—she could remember coming for dinner here the night of her senior prom—and stepped into the kitchen. The carpenters were both there, their backs to her, as they fit a piece of Sheetrock in one of the walls. She saw another door just inside the room. She gently tugged the handle but found it wouldn't budge. Would they keep the cellar locked?

The old door had a skeleton key sitting right in the keyhole. She guessed she would find out. One of the carpenters had turned sideways as he pushed the Sheetrock in place. She needed to move quickly before he saw her out of the corner of his eye. No one would stop her now. She turned the key and opened the door, stepping inside and shutting the door behind her.

"Karen?" she heard someone ask outside.

She guessed that was the name of one of the owners. So they hadn't really seen her, maybe only caught a glimpse of her skirt as she closed the door.

She was breathing hard. She needed to calm down. She was in total darkness. She couldn't see a thing. If there was a light switch, where would it be? She felt along the right hand wall. *There!*

She flipped on the switch and was rewarded with a single lightbulb, glowing up at her from the bottom of the stairs. She had found the cellar. She would find her boy.

"I'm coming for you, baby," she whispered, as she started down the stairs. She almost stumbled. The stairs were old wooden slats, cracked in places. They creaked under her weight. She shouldn't go too fast. She wished she had something to steady her nerves.

She paused, trying to control her breathing again. She thought she heard something down below, a faint, mewling noise, like some animal in pain.

Phyllis didn't want to talk too loud. She didn't want anybody to know she was down here until she had gotten a good look around.

"Hello?" she called softly.

The noise repeated itself, a little louder than before.

"Hello?" she said, in a conversational tone, now. She could hear hammering come from up above. Anybody upstairs wouldn't be able to hear anything else.

"Is anybody here?" she added.

"Mum-mum," the voice repeated. It was a voice, she was sure of it. But she could hear it was in pain.

"Who are you?" she called. "Do you need help?"

"Mum-mah," the voice replied, as if struggling to form words. She knew that voice. Didn't she?

"Kenny?" she called out, even louder than before. Who cared if they found her, if she could rescue her son.

"Mommy?" the voice cried clearly, just as her son had called her, so very long ago.

"Where are you?" she yelled. He hadn't called her Mommy since he was seven. Something must be very wrong.

"Mommy! Here! Mommy!"

Even with the single lightbulb, she could tell he was nowhere in the small cellar room. She heard a rustling sound. Was he caught someplace? Couldn't he get out?

"Kenny!"

She heard the rustling again. It was coming from a three-foot crawl space, just beyond the main room. The space was entirely lost in shadow.

Could Kenny be hurt? Could he have crawled in there to feel safe? She thought of all the times over the years when she had let her boy down, when she couldn't be there for him; the time she ran off before Kenny's father had died, and later on, those nights when she hadn't come home at all. But she was here now. She'd make up for all those other times. She'd keep him safe, and they would be together forever.

"I'm coming for you baby," she said again.

One of her shoes gave way beneath her. She almost stumbled forward against the dark opening. She heard the rustling again. Was Kenny coming toward her? She had heard another, softer sound as well, a faint hiss. Air escaping from an old inner tube or something. Heaven knew what they kept stored back there. The sound had reminded her a little of a snake.

She looked down at her feet. Her heel had caught on the uneven floor and snapped completely off. She should have changed her shoes from the bar last night. But she wasn't going to let anything stop her now. She kicked off her other shoe as well. She would rescue her son in her stocking feet.

"Kenny?" she called, softer now.

"Closer, Mommy, closer."

She placed one hand on the edge of the crawl space. It was so dark in there, she couldn't see a thing.

"Why don't you come out here, honey? Come out where Mommy can see you?"

"I'm right here, Mommy, right here."

"Where baby?" She leaned her full weight against the ledge of the crawl space now. Did she see two points of light in the darkness, two eyes reflecting the light behind her?

She reached into the darkness. Her fingers felt something damp, like rotting leaves.

"Kenny?" she called.

The eyes came toward her very quickly.

She screamed when she saw that they weren't eyes after all.

SIXTEEN

"One of the best locations is coming up on our left," Angela called from the backseat.

Thomas P. Dalton II attempted to look mildly interested, but he wasn't used to being a passenger. His daughter's plans for the underutilized space in town made sense. It was a beautiful location, and people would pay for new construction in the middle of all this history. He was sure that the company could make a tidy profit from the venture. He had let her lay out her plans without comment. She was a smart woman, even when she was preparing to stab him in the back. Once this project got started, he might even let Angela control the details, with John as her assistant. At least for a while.

"As you can see," his daughter said, "there's a small restaurant on the property."

A neon sign read "Sid's Clam Shack." The building

itself, two rooms long with a take-out window at one end, was badly in need of a coat of paint.

"The restaurant is a few blocks too far north of the most popular area of town, and only does a really strong business in the summer, maybe three months of the year. In other words, it is not a high-profit enterprise. I believe we can get the owner to sell for a reasonable fee. Converted to housing, this parcel becomes much more valuable, especially with its proximity to the ocean."

The Atlantic was only a block away. This was prime real estate. Angela was stating the obvious.

His mind would wander from time to time. Usually to thoughts of Emily. It was odd. After the separation, he had been able to drive her from his mind for long periods of time and focus his attention on their children. Since she had died, though, she seemed to be in his thoughts with increasingly frequency. Especially at those moments when his body let him down and he was forced to rest. His past would come flooding back. How excited he was when he won her. How proud he was to walk into an event with her on his arm. How angry he became when she wouldn't listen to reason.

Ralph turned his car off the beach road. Thomas looked out at the houses on the back streets; smaller cottages here, rather than the larger Victorians at the center of town. Apparently, this part of the tour was over. Angela began praising the restaurant where they would go for lunch.

He would let them take the lead for now. He knew he had to make some changes. Nothing happened in this company without his knowing every detail. Everyone ultimately reported to him. No exceptions, even with Angela's special plans.

He would string them along with all their transparent schemes. How could he promise his son the Abbadon and then take it away? He was sure he would come up with a way; some fine print in the contract, a talk to the local banks to refuse a loan, some company reorganization that would nullify a handshake agreement that he could somehow no longer remember. There would be a hundred ways to accomplish that sort of thing. He relished seeing the look of defeat on John's face when his son realized who would always be in control.

Sometimes he could see Emily's face reflected in his youngest son. When John really frowned, he could almost see Emily's tears. He saw bits of her in all three children, but John, who had stayed with her the longest, most held her mark.

Emily had defeated him, for a little while at least. Why did she have to be so willful? But he was never vanquished for long. And he wouldn't be second to anyone.

He knew John was trying to run away, that Angela was trying to manipulate her old man. They thought he was too old to notice, too old to fight back.

He wasn't young anymore. But he would fight until the moment he died.

Who knew how much longer he had? He had had moments of weakness, when his heart could no longer keep up with his desires. His will had been stronger than his illness, at least so far. His doctors urged him to slow down, as though that was an option.

Maybe he'd get Tip down here, get the whole family

together. Maybe he would make this his great final statement of control, so that none of them would ever forget who was their father.

See, Emily? See what you force me to do?

Angela was still talking. "Those six properties, the five I've showed you and the Abbadon, will form the core of our initial effort. There are two more lots a little outside of town that I'd like to consider for Phase Two. I'll have Ralph take you up there after lunch."

"But not the Abbadon?" Thomas shot back.

"I told you. The moving van's there today. We've agreed to meet John and his wife there tomorrow."

Angela had already told him this at least three times. He just liked to watch her squirm.

He looked out the window. "You know what's best, I suppose."

"I never thought I'd get you to admit it."

Well, he didn't really believe it, now, did he? But a little flattery was good now and then.

"I'll give it one more day. Then it's back to New York on Saturday."

He would let them take him to lunch, take it easy for a bit before he made his play. Once he got away from Angela, he'd put an end to this nonsense once and for all.

He was going to pay an early visit to the Abbadon. This afternoon. He would simply tell Ralph to turn around and drive him where he wanted to go.

Ralph had to obey him. He wasn't family.

Karen walked into the kitchen to see how Eddie and Stan were doing. They had torn down one whole corner of the room and about twenty square feet of flooring. The space behind the wall reminded Karen a bit of the third floor. Some of the exposed wood looked only a few years old; other pieces looked like they might have been there for a hundred years.

"We're almost done for the day," Eddie said. "We'll leave you in peace pretty soon."

He waved at what they had ripped apart.

"Most of the stuff behind the walls is still pretty sturdy. We're going to have to replace some of the sub-floor right around where they had the fire, build a new frame for that wall over there, lay down a new hardwood floor in this corner that will match the existing boards. Barring any last minute surprises, we should be done with this by the middle of next week."

"And we can have a working kitchen." Karen smiled at that. That's what happened when you ate out for weeks on end. She was actually looking forward to cooking again. And John liked to bake; making elaborate concoctions relaxed him. Maybe they could experiment with some things in the weeks before they opened for business.

"It was pretty crazy in here today, huh?" Eddie said.

Karen nodded. "Since the movers have gone, it's gotten quiet."

"Amazing what losing half a dozen people clomping around can do. We were hearing all sorts of noises back here. Stan even thought he heard somebody scream."

"A scream?" Karen asked.

"Probably kids outside." Stan nodded. "These old houses can carry noise in weird ways."

The phone rang in the lobby. They would have to get

an extension back here. This place was too big to go
running after phone calls. It stopped two and a half
rings in. John must have gotten it. Stan went back to
measuring something on the floor.

"So did you tell him?" Eddie asked softly.

Karen nodded. "I think he's still in shock."

She didn't mention any of John's comments about
Eddie. If she was ever subconsciously going in that direction, it was over now.

"Oh, there you are."

She turned around. John stood in the door to the dining room.

"Angela called. She's meeting me down at the lunch-
eonette on the beach."

"Does she have good news?"

"Well, she says my father's not being as difficult as
she had expected. She's not sure if that's a good sign.
She just wanted to compare notes before we all got together tomorrow."

He waved for Karen to follow him into the dining
room. Once she got there, he shut the kitchen door behind her.

"I'm going to tell her we have another source of
capital."

"Really?" Karen was pleasantly surprised.

"My father's going to play hardball. We might as
well, too."

"Well, I hope it goes well."

"Thanks." He gave her a quick hug and a kiss. "I
should be back in an hour or two."

"I'll lock up here, make sure everything's shipshape."
She wondered if she should volunteer to go along. But

John looked like he wanted to do this on his own. She didn't want to do anything to undermine his newfound strength. Besides, according to their agreement, when he got back he'd have to tell her all about it.

Karen walked him out to the front door. He waved as he headed toward the beach.

How things could turn around. She felt as if they had been on the verge of their biggest argument ever. Instead, she felt closer to him than she had in years.

She stood in the doorway for a long moment, staring out toward the ocean. You couldn't quite see the Atlantic from here, the angle was wrong. Other houses blocked the way. But the sea was the whole reason Cape May was here, the reason they could reopen this inn. She had thought, when they first came to town, that they would take walks along the beach every day. That was one more thing that hadn't happened. In the weeks they had been in and out of town, they had walked by the sea—what, maybe twice? That was something else she would like to change. Something else she and John could talk about.

She heard boots clomping down the hall behind her. She turned around to see Stan and Eddie approaching, toolboxes in their hands.

"We can't come tomorrow, but we'll see you Monday," Eddie said as he passed by her. "I left the plans for the hotel on the kitchen counter."

She waved good-bye and watched them leave in their truck. After all those people in the Abbadon today, she was now completely alone. The workers had started the renovations, the movers had come and gone. She guessed they could now really claim the Abbadon as their own. She still couldn't believe this place was theirs. She wondered if she ever would.

No, that was negative thinking. She and John were going to work things out. This was the place they were going to call their home.

She resisted an impulse to check on the money. Once the movers were gone, she had found a space to hide the envelope in one of the boxes. It was safe enough there for now. For the long term, maybe she should go with tradition and stuff it under the mattress.

For now, Karen decided she wanted to go back and look at that other wall—that odd mix of wood and stone and brick that now lay exposed in the kitchen—while no one was around. She had found the wall fascinating when the carpenters had uncovered it before, with bits of maybe half a dozen former versions of the inn hidden inside. It was as if that wall was the secret inner heart of the Abbadon.

She walked through the empty inn. It was getting dark out. The long windows let in hardly any light. It must be well past four by now, and the clouds made the dusk come that much earlier. How long was John going to be gone? Another hour, she guessed.

Something wasn't right in the dining room. She stopped for a moment, halfway through. Her footsteps didn't sound right on the worn carpet. The air felt a little colder in here. The fading light threw the corners of the room into shadow. It was nothing, really. It was as if there was just something—off.

Did she hear a noise—a thumping, like a rubber ball bouncing down a set of stairs? She pushed open the door to the kitchen.

She saw it, right in front of her. The cellar door was open. A blast of cold air hit her in the face, as if the basement was opened to the outside air.

Karen frowned. The cellar door had been locked the last time she was in the kitchen.

Was someone down there? Had Stan or Eddie come back? The movers were long gone. Had John decided not to meet with Angela? Had he gone down to check the furnace instead?

"Hello?" she called.

She heard a high, whistling sound, like a teapot just starting to steam.

"Hello?" she called again.

The whistling ceased abruptly. She heard nothing. The silence somehow seemed very deep. She found herself leaning forward, almost as if she might fall into the basement before her.

The cellar door slammed in her face.

Karen jumped back. The wind did strange things in this place. Apparently it opened and closed doors all by itself, too. She waited for a minute, listening for any sounds from downstairs. The house was utterly still.

She locked the basement door again. She was glad she didn't have to go down into the cellar. That was one job that John could keep.

She walked carefully around the exposed floor, made sure the back door was locked and all the windows were closed. By the time John got back from his meeting, she would be ready to go.

She turned to look at the wall. It was almost like some abstract sculpture. The base of the wall had brick running along the left-hand side, stones and mortar running along the right. The two support beams closest to the other walls looked old, but the center one was as dark as obsidian. Those other beams sported cross beams, nails, old wires, bits of insulation, but nothing else was attached floor to ceiling, to the dark wood at the center. It was quite striking. She reached out to touch it but pulled back her hand. It would be more fun to leave it a mystery.

She walked back through the dining room, headed toward the apartment and the piles of boxes. Sooner or later, this would be their living space. Boxes and furniture were piled to either side of the main room, leaving only a six-foot-wide passage down the middle. As far as this room was concerned, sooner was not an option.

Maybe if she just dealt with one or two of the boxes at a time. Perhaps put aside the bathroom stuff for when they actually moved over here—something practical like that. She knew she would feel better if she made a dent in the pile. They would check out of their motel on Sunday, the end of their weekly rate, and bring all the rest of their belongings over. She would like to have a place to put those, too.

She couldn't believe how exhausted she was. Maybe she needed to sit down for a minute first.

John would be back soon. They could go out for dinner.

It would be great when they could make their first dinner here. John liked to cook for relaxation. She wondered if he really could do it for their guests.

Hell, they were going to be able to do everything.

Where was John, anyway? It would be getting really dark out soon. She didn't want to have to get mad at him all over again.

She walked past the living room into the bedroom. The movers had set this room up, bureaus, night tables, and all, so they could immediately use it.

And they had a bed. Maybe she'd sleep right here.

Of course, she had to put it together.

She had been very methodical about marking the boxes. She quickly found the sheets and blankets—the movers had stacked them at the very front of the pile—then the comforter—in the box below—and carefully made up the bed. The lights hadn't made it onto the nightstands. She would use a desk lamp if she wanted to read.

She opened a box of books to get something to read. All the comforts of home, she thought.

She heard the wind, keening softly through a loose window pane. The inn always had its little sounds. This was certainly less strident than that wailing she had heard in the kitchen. After a while, she imagined she would get used to all of them. There would be different sounds, too, once they got guests in here, and hired a couple of people to help with the cleaning and maybe spell them on the front desk. This really felt like it could be a working business.

But her exhaustion wasn't going away. Well, what the heck. She could take a little nap. She would wake up when John got back.

She kicked off her shoes.

It felt like the greatest luxury in the world to climb into her own bed.

The wind sighed softly on the other side of the windows. It was a relaxing sound, almost as if she was being serenaded to sleep.

For the first time, she really could see how she might be able to call this place home.

John should be here soon. She was looking forward to the two of them sharing their own bed.

She couldn't read. Her eyes were heavy.

The wind whispered.

Just a few minutes, then.

She half expected him to call if he was going to be late.

She dreamed she was walking the halls. The hotel looked like new. It was full of guests.

She drifted in and out of sleep.

She heard the rustle of sheets, felt the tug of blankets.

"John?" she murmured.

It was very sweet to have him climb into bed with her. They would take a little nap together. She smiled in her sleep.

He must have brought some of the air from outside with him. Something felt very cold. For an instant, she wanted to wake up.

She was drifting.

She was out beyond the Abbadon. The ocean had picked her up. Or maybe it was the wind. She could see all of Cape May spread out before her. The whole town was sleeping and dark. Only one house was lit. No, not a house. It was the Abbadon Inn. It wasn't an ordinary light, either. The illumination was a ghostly blue, as cold as the frost in winter.

Karen struggled to open her eyes.

She wasn't alone in the room.

She couldn't tell if this was a dream or not.

"John?" she called. She heard the word aloud.

She thought she heard him call her name in response. No, the name wasn't Karen. Another name.

Lucy.

She knew that name. From where? If only she could climb out of her dream. But her sleep was too deep. She heard the sheets rustle at her side.

She shivered for a minute, then fell back asleep.

The Abbadon Inn was the center of everything. And she was once again rising above it, rising above the town, the ocean, the world. Anything in life, and beyond life, was hers for the asking.

"John?" she asked again.

She got no answer.

It didn't matter. Cape May was hers.

SEVENTEEN

Thomas P. Dalton II glared over at his son-in-law from where he sat in the passenger seat of the car.

"You know exactly what I want."

Ralph smiled mildly. He never ever seemed to get ruffled. In Manhattan, Thomas had admired that in the man. Now he found it annoying.

"This farmland is a real steal." Ralph repeated what Angela wanted him to say. "This close to the ocean, and all that vacation business, we could build a thirty-six-hole golf course and a couple hundred units of vacation housing."

"I believe you." He continued to watch his son-in-law. "Well, actually, I believe Angela. I know she always does her homework. I don't need to see the fields, or the location. I need to see the Abbadon Inn."

Ralph sighed. "You know it would be easier on all of us if you waited until tomorrow."

"I never got anywhere in the business world by being easy. I got where I am by acting quickly, decisively, when I was ready. If you want to continue working for my firm, you will take me to the Abbadon."

Ralph raised his eyebrows. "Won't Angela have something to say about that?"

"I know, if I threaten you, she threatens me. That balance of power doesn't work anymore. If I have to, I'll replace you all. I came here to see the Abbadon, and I won't be delayed another minute!"

"But—" Ralph began.

"Not one more word! We're going to the Abbadon."

Thomas smiled as Ralph turned the car around.

Ralph had delayed the old man as long as he could. He had taken the long way around on the way back home, adding an extra half hour on their journey back to town. He had hoped that Thomas would get tired, or distracted, or come up with some idea more important than the Abbadon. But when Thomas Dalton got focused, he was like a bulldog with a raw steak. Actually, put old Dalton in a tug-of-war for the steak, and Ralph pitied the bulldog.

So they were headed for the Abbadon.

He wished he could find a phone, get through to Angela. But he didn't even know where she would be, out for coffee with her brother, or back at the hotel. She might even be at the Abbadon herself. He hoped they would find her at the inn. She'd find a way to handle the old man.

Cape May looked a little drab tonight. The clouds were bringing dusk in early. Everything was a uniform gray. Ralph parked across the street from the inn.

"This is what you wanted," he announced. "The Abbadon Inn."

"At last!" Thomas actually cackled with glee. "What say we take the tour?"

They strode across the street side by side. Ralph remembered the last time he had been to this place; the bad sensation he had gotten as he walked the inn's halls. He hoped his feelings had been a reaction to the stress of Angela finally making a sort of peace with her brother. He hoped the things he had felt were only his imagination.

He had not particularly looked forward to coming back here. Especially not as a tour guide for Thomas P. Dalton.

It was very quiet on the street. No one walking. Not a single car. Where was everybody? It wasn't even five o'clock.

The front door was wide open.

"I guess they were expecting us," Thomas said as he stepped inside.

Ralph walked inside the lobby and closed the door behind him. It was very still in here. The movers must be done. He guessed the carpenters were gone for the day as well. If John was still with Angela, that probably meant that Karen was here by herself.

"Karen!" Ralph called.

"Quiet!" Thomas demanded in a loud whisper. "Let's take a look around here first."

Ralph suppressed a shiver. The sensations he had had before were even stronger this time around. A sense of unease, of something else being here, something watching him, watching both of them, and waiting. Waiting for what? And now Thomas wanted to sneak around? Maybe Ralph should go back to the car and let the old man get lost in here.

He wouldn't, of course, through some strange sense of responsibility. Thomas was his father-in-law, after all.

They walked out of the lobby and passed the staircase.

Thomas paused. "Did you hear that? Someone's upstairs."

Ralph hadn't heard anything.

Thomas looked up and down the hall as he scratched at the back of his neck. "This is quite a big place. I'm surprised they could afford it. I'm actually a little impressed." He looked back at Ralph. "I'll fire you if you breathe a word of that to John."

Still his same bitter, hateful self. He had always seen that in Thomas, Ralph thought, but age was changing him. Ever since he had started having those heart attacks. Some people, when they see the end, want to make amends, right some of the wrongs that have gone before. Not Thomas P. Dalton II. These last months, the civilized veneer had stripped away, leaving only the rotten core.

Ralph was surprised no one else in the family had said anything. Maybe his family didn't see it. It was not Ralph's place to bring it up. He liked everybody else to think of him as the quiet guy. It gave him a chance to listen. But he always held his own opinions.

The old man looked back up the stairs.

"Did you hear that voice?"

Ralph still hadn't heard a thing.

"Sometimes old structures make noises," he said reasonably. "Sometimes around here, old houses have ghosts." Their hotel manager had been talking about that just the other morning. He had heard Karen mention something about that when they had lunch the other day, In the middle of the day, ghosts had seemed romantic. Now, all he could think about were eyes in the walls.

"Someone's trying to hide on me. Well, I'm livelier than they think." Thomas headed up the steps.

"I haven't been up here before," Ralph called as he reluctantly followed. He flicked a light switch at the base of the stairs. Light spilled down from above. "We only looked around the first floor."

"Wow, this is quite some place," Thomas called down from above. "It's going to take some real fixing up. I can see why they need the money. You can't charge first-class rates without first-class accommodations."

Ralph reached the second floor at last. The old man was already going from room to room, looking in the open doors. He was getting excited, like some kid playing hide and seek. "So who's up here? Why don't you come out so we can talk?"

He looked around sharply. "Upstairs!" he headed for the stairs to the third floor. "It looks like I get my exercise today."

Ralph had heard the faintest of sounds. Maybe a voice, maybe only the creak of floorboards overhead. He flipped another switch at the landing. A much fainter illumination came down from the third floor.

"Hello?" The old man was sounding impatient. "Come out. Come out now!"

Ralph came up the steps behind him.

Thomas jumped a bit when Ralph put a hand on his shoulder.

"It's a little dark up here." He scanned the ceiling. "I don't see any other lights."

Even in the shadows, Ralph could see some of the walls had been torn apart. Across the hall, it looked like a new wall was being built.

Thomas laughed through his nose. "Guess they won't be letting out rooms on this floor anytime soon."

Ralph could hear something. Or feel something. He wasn't quite sure. Not quite a voice. Something that would pretend to be a voice. It might be saying a word. It might even be saying *Thomas.*

"Stop calling my name and show yourself!"

Ralph could sense it moving. Whatever it was, it was no longer content to watch. Now it was coming straight toward them.

"Over there!" Thomas called.

There was something in the shadows that threatened to turn into a human shape.

Ralph felt like it was right on top of them.

"There you are! John, is that you? I thought I'd come up and surprise you. Why don't you come out, and we can talk."

The face was lost in the shadows for a moment, and then seemed to materialize right in front of Thomas.

It wasn't John. It was a woman's face. It was hard for Ralph to see her clearly. Her skin was almost too bright against the darkness.

"Oh, my god." Thomas whispered. He stumbled back.

The woman vanished, as if the old man's reaction had scared her away.

"What?" Ralph demanded. What had he seen?

Thomas was shaking his head. "It can't be right. It just can't be." He turned to Ralph. "Did you see anything?"

"A woman, maybe," Ralph replied. "It's dark up here. I couldn't be sure."

Thomas nodded his head. "Dark up here. That's it. What was I thinking?"

Thomas was breathing heavily. Ralph wondered if all this exercise was too much for the old man.

"Maybe we'd better sit down," he suggested. There was probably a chair somewhere.

"No!" Thomas replied vehemently. "Down the stairs. I'll be much better once I'm down the stairs."

"Okay. Why don't you lean on me. We'll go down easy."

It was only when Thomas took Ralph's arm that he realized that the old man was shaking. They started down the stairs together, slowly, one step, then the next.

They made it to the second floor. Ralph realized he was breathing more easily. The sensation, so strong on the floor above, was growing more and more distant. Whatever it was, it wasn't following them.

"Need to rest," Thomas gasped. They stood for a long moment on the landing, the stairs down to the first floor only a few feet away.

Maybe this place had scared Thomas out of whatever he was going to do. Ralph would prefer if he never had to set foot inside it again.

"What now?" Ralph asked at last.

Thomas didn't say a thing. He looked back at the stairway that led to the third floor.

"I think we'd better go," Ralph prompted after a moment.

"It's late," the old man replied, his breathing more under control. "Perhaps you're right. But we're coming back here. There's no way they're keeping me away from here."

Oh, dear, Ralph thought. He had no idea what had gotten into the old man's head. He hoped Angela wouldn't be too mad at him.

Don hadn't gone to a doctor. Janet would have found out somehow, and he would never hear the end of it.

He had bought a bottle instead. Gladys was out at one of her prayer meetings. That damned church was taking up her life. Well, that and taking care of J.J.

The boy had actually seemed a little better lately. Having other people see something down in that basement appeared to help him. Janet had taken the boy over to a classmate's house to work on a science project. She would pick him up when her meeting was done. They would both be home a little after nine.

That gave Don a couple of hours of freedom. He liked to think of it as quality time. He looked at the bottle of vodka. The good stuff. He would only allow himself a little at a time, to get him through until his arm started to get better.

He didn't want to think about the dead spots. His arm had to get better. He had to believe it.

Don smiled. He was beginning to sound like his wife.

He stared back at the bottle with a frown. Didn't he used to be master of this house? Now here he was, sneaking around behind Janet's back, just to get a little comfort.

A man has his needs. Not that Janet ever looked at him that way anymore. Well, hardly ever. When was the last time they had gotten that close? Once, during Christmas week. It had been so long since they'd been together that it had felt awkward, forced. When it was over, they hadn't said a word.

Fuck it all. A man needed more attention than a couple major holidays. Maybe he needed to go back out by himself again. That always used to start the fights around here, all those long nights when he use to hit the bars. Well, maybe it was time for another fight or two.

The hell with it. He needed something warm in his belly. He poured an inch in the bottom of his glass, and took it down in a single swallow.

Donny.

That was the women used to call him, before he got married. Dandy Donny. Man, but they'd had their fun back then. He had known some pretty wild women in his time. And Janet had been just about as wild as any of them.

Donny?

He thought he heard somebody. Somebody he had known a long time ago. Just his imagination. His imagination and vodka.

The voice in his head had sounded a little bit like Phyllis. The old Phyllis. The happy Phyllis. Before life had dragged her down.

Janet never liked Phyllis in the first place. Don half

thought that was the reason Phyllis and he had ended up sleeping together. He certainly knew it would get back to his wife eventually. In a place like Cape May, the locals knew everything.

That was a few years back, before Phyllis had let herself go. She had been a fine-looking woman back then. He had had Phyllis call him Donny sometimes. It made him feel young. Being with her had made Don feel like he was twenty.

He shook his head. The arm, the one with the dead spots, felt like it was falling asleep. He flexed his fingers to get the circulation going and poured himself just a little more.

Phyllis had let the booze get to her. He would never let that happen to him.

He stared at his hand. His fingers were tingling.

Don looked up. He'd heard a noise, like somebody was tapping on the window. It was probably just a tree branch, pushed by the winter wind.

There it was—*tic tic tic, tic tic tic.* It had a regular rhythm, like somebody was trying to get his attention.

Don got up from the desk and opened the window. The winter cold hit him like a slap in the face.

Donny! a woman's voice said quite clearly.

"Who's out there?" he called.

The woman laughed. It was a very inviting sound.

Has it been that long?

He knew that voice. It was really her. "Phyllis?"

I knew you'd remember.

He peered out into the darkness. "What are you doing out there? Where are you?"

She stepped into the glow of a streetlight, just outside

the Abbadon next door. She was wearing one of those tight dresses she used to favor. Shouldn't she be wearing a coat?

A part of Don was glad she wasn't.

She looked much better than he had seen her in years. He wondered if she was trying to sober up.

Donny. I wanted to thank you. She smiled at him, a warm, inviting smile. *I found Kenny at last. I couldn't have done it without you.*

"What do you mean?"

The cellar. I got in there. Kenny had left me something in the cellar.

He guessed he was happy for her. These days, Kenny was about all she had left.

I know Janet isn't home. I thought maybe we could talk. Like we used to.

He couldn't let her in. What if Janet got home early? But what harm would there be if he went out in the yard and chatted for a bit?

"Wait a minute!" he called. "I'll come on out."

He grabbed a light coat on his way. Just because Phyllis was a little crazy didn't mean Don had to catch his death. He paused at the door, went back to his desk, and took a final shot.

For luck.

He scratched absently at his arm. The dead spots were itching like crazy. They were coming back to life.

Maybe Phyllis could bring some other parts of him back to life as well. He would have to hustle her out of here, maybe find a motel room out of town. Should he have left a note for Janet, come up with some excuse?

He was getting ahead of himself here. He had to talk to Phyllis first and see where that led.

What if Janet found out? Don paused, just before he opened the back door. What did it matter? How much love was left in their marriage anyway?

She only had time for the latest craze, from cutting coupons to Christian Science. These days, whatever made Janet feel better consumed her.

He stepped out on the lawn. Phyllis walked toward him along the narrow space that separated Don's house from the Abbadon.

Her smile was brilliant in the half-dark. She looked better than she had in years. He had forgotten how attractive she could be.

"You're looking great," he said as he walked to meet her.

Donny, she replied. *I so wanted you to come out.*

"Have you stopped drinking?" he asked, and immediately thought, what a stupid thing to say!

Oh, I've found something much better than drinking. She reached her arms out toward him. *Donny, honey, you look good enough to eat.*

She looked like she wanted to do it here.

"Hey, we've got to go someplace," he began.

She laughed. *Donny, I've already got the place picked out.*

This was great news, but not here, not now. Phyllis was crowding him a bit, getting closer. He took a step back, and was surprised when his heel hit something hard rather than the mushy ground of the winter lawn. He looked down and saw that he had stepped onto the sidewalk behind the Abbadon. He looked along the side of the old hotel. The basement door was open, only a few feet away.

Somewhere, not too far away, he heard a car door slam.

He thought he heard his wife calling his name.

She couldn't find him like this! He had to get back into the house.

"I'm sorry, Phyllis. Maybe we can talk some other time." He tried to slide on by her.

She stepped forward to block his path. *You're going to leave me so soon?*

"We'll find some place to talk," he said hurriedly, looking for a way around her. "Away from here. Maybe tomorrow."

But she wasn't listening. *Everybody leaves Phyllis. I can't let another one go. I'm not alone. I'll never be alone again.* She looked at him again with her dazzling smile. *And neither will you.* Her teeth were very white, but her eyes were as dark as the night.

"What are you saying?" Don retreated a couple more steps. "I have to go home. You can't stop me!"

Kenny will help me.

Her smile became impossibly wide as a shorter shape stepped out from behind her. It was the size of a twelve-year-old, but it didn't look like Kenny. It didn't even look human.

Kenny and so many more. She brushed the back of his hand with her own. Her touch felt like ice.

When he looked back at Phyllis, she didn't look exactly human, either.

He felt a jolt as Kenny's cold hand tightened around his wrist. The cold seemed to spread out from his arm until it reached through every inch of his body.

Don pulled away. "I'm not coming with you!" His teeth were chattering as he tried to speak.

That just made Phyllis laugh.

Donny, darling! You're already there!

He tried to cry out as the weight pushed against him. He no longer had a voice. Something covered his face as he fell down the cellar steps.

EIGHTEEN

John found Karen asleep in their bed. He had heard her muttering as he came into their bedroom. It sounded as if she was having a nightmare.

She cried out as he came into the room.

"Honey, honey, it's all right. I'm here." He put a hand gently on her shoulder.

She opened one eye to look up at him. "John. I'm so glad you're here." She gave him a sleepy grin. "I was going to take a little nap."

She sat up, shaking her head and blinking.

"I had a dream," she said after a moment. "It had something to do with Jack Cooney. He's the man who wrote the letters. The letters in the box."

She frowned, looking down at the bed.

"Did you just get back here?"

He sat down on the bed beside her. "Maybe five minutes ago. I went looking in the kitchen for you first."

"I thought I heard . . . or maybe I felt . . ." She shook her head again. "I think I'm still half asleep."

"You looked so comfortable there. It made me feel like this really is our home." He took a minute to look around the room. "We could stay here. Maybe order some take-out. You've got things set up pretty well."

She shook her head. "No. All our clothing and stuff's back at the motel. Let's go back, get some of our things together in the morning. We'll be over here soon enough."

She paused again. "What a strange dream."

"About some guy named Jack?"

"I've just been reading his letters. I guess in a way I've been seeing this place through his eyes." She looked up at John. "Were you ever called Jack?"

He laughed. "In my family? You've got to be kidding."

"It is funny about the names." She shrugged. "I'm going to get up. I locked up the hotel pretty well before I fell asleep. The cellar door was open again."

John frowned. "Did you need to go down there?"

"The wind whipped the door shut before I got to it. I half felt like the hotel was keeping me out." She laughed. "That comes from reading Jack Cooney's letters. I'm going to bring them along tonight. I'll read you the best parts." She threw the covers off and stood. "My shoes are around here somewhere. Oh!" She looked up at her husband. "What happened with Angela?"

John shrugged. "Well, she's got some good plans. We'll have to see if Dad will let them happen."

"Here they are!" She scooped up her sneakers, then stepped over and kissed John on the cheek. "No. We're

going to make things happen. I know we will." She
smiled. "What do you say to that?"

"I think I know a woman who deserves to be taken
out to dinner." He held out his elbow. "If you'll take my
arm, I'll escort you to one of the finest burger places in
town."

"Such a gentleman," she replied.

They left the Abbadon arm in arm.

Karen really wanted to look at the letters. But she
needed to let John finish his explanation first.

"So Angela's going to place all the holdings down
here under a separate trust," he continued, waving his
fork in the air for emphasis, "not immediately under my
father's control. Oh, there will still be ways for him to
influence things, but it will be a tremendous pain in the
rear to do so. And Angela's figuring my father just
doesn't have the time to do much of that."

"It makes sense," she agreed.

John nodded. "With my father's current health, she
doesn't think he'll be around all that much longer. She's
looking for all sorts of ways to pick up the pieces after
he's gone.

"That sounds a little coldhearted."

"Hey. It's a proud Dalton tradition."

John pushed away his carton of noodles. "I think I'm
full. And satisfied."

She smiled back at him. "I think we're both satisfied." She had to admit, this was the most relaxed she
had felt since coming to the Jersey Shore.

They had gotten take-out after all. On their walk

back from the Abbadon, they had both decided they'd rather have the privacy of their room.

It was like an unspoken agreement. They had agreed to work together. They had agreed to be close again.

They got into the room. The food had been pushed into a corner, and their clothes had come off as soon as John had shut the door behind them. They had had the best sex since they had come to Cape May, and maybe months before that.

"We'll have to do that again soon," John had said to her when they were done. "In our own bed, in our new home."

"We will." She was just as glad they had waited to come back here. The dream she had had back at the hotel was still creeping her out.

Once they had satisfied their lust, it was finally time for dinner. The Chinese could no longer be called hot. But lukewarm *mu-shu* was still pretty good, especially considering what went before.

She glanced through the next letter while John went to the bathroom. It was another good one. She was glad she was sharing these with him now. She no longer had to keep the letters, or a lot of things, to herself.

She had told him something about the earlier letters as they had walked back to the motel. How some of the notes talked about the history of Cape May and the local belief in ghosts—and how some of the letters had barely been letters at all. And how one of them had led to their cash windfall.

She heard the toilet, then running water as John washed his hands. She looked up as he walked back into the room.

"Are you ready for a little correspondence?"

"Sounds better than TV," he replied.

She unfolded the letter before her with a flourish.

"This one's all about the history of the hotel. I read ahead a bit. There's parts of this that show the Abbadon's dark side."

John grinned. "We have a dark side? Would that make people want to stay away?"

"I think it would make people want to stay all the more. It's adventurous. This stuff may sound a little dangerous, but really, it's just an old inn."

John nodded. "Maybe we should do a brochure."

"Well, wait until you hear this first." She smoothed the letter out on the desk and began to read.

Dear Lucy,

Well, if you're going to stay someplace, I guess it might as well be famous. There sure is a lot of local press about the Abbadon Inn.

And not just the uproar about Tito planning to tear it down. It appears this place has always attracted controversy. I got into a discussion with one of the librarians. If you go into the library often enough, they start to say hello.

So we got to talking. She said it was far from the first time the Abbadon's been in the news. She steered me toward these old books and newspapers.

The most famous, and reputable thing about this hotel was the restaurant. Often advertised in the weekly paper, it was called "The Orchid." It was the place to dine in Cape May. And no matter how many different people owned this place, the name was always the same. I think Tito's going to use the name again once he gets the place up and running.

But I'm getting ahead of myself again.

I've come across some local histories. Many of them are self-published, or put out by some academic press that you've never heard of. Most of these local histories are badly written (or in the case of the academic volumes, overwritten). But they all at least mention the Abbadon. At least three of them have whole chapters on the inn.

The accounts vary, and some of the stories are pretty wild. Still, there are certain common threads, and a couple things that are so juicy I just want to believe them, whether they really happened or not.

I believe there was always a house on this property, ever since Cape May was run by a bunch of whaling families back around the Revolutionary War. The current structure, much smaller than it is now, was first built as an inn, maybe sometime in the 1850s and run by a gentleman of Greek descent named Nicholas Abbadon—thus the name.

Eventually, he began to run the place with a woman, referred to only as Lillith. When she showed up isn't exactly clear. Whether or not Lillith was his wife is not exactly clear. It's interesting that all the books seem equally hazy about this.

But old Nicholas wasn't satisfied with his simple inn. Cape May was booming, and the Abbadon was going to grow along with it. A new inn was built around the original structure—the building that would become the inn as we know it. An architect named Stephen Decatur Button, who apparently was a pretty big deal at the time, designed the big Victorian that we're now trying to restore.

The construction, interestingly, was reportedly plagued by accidents. A number of the workers lost their lives in the months it took to rebuild this place. The local papers reported on it, but not in any great detail. Maybe these sort of mishaps were more common in those days. Most of the workmen were guys just off the boats from Europe—cheap labor, and easily replaced. But the building took far longer to renovate than anyone had imagined.

On top of that, the man in charge of rebuilding (either the architect, or perhaps his foreman, the writing is unclear) seemed to have gotten an odd, withering illness, perhaps contracted on a visit to the Indies, but he never quite saw the end of construction. Or perhaps the Abbadon Inn was never quite finished. Again, the histories are unclear. I certainly know there are parts of it that need to be rebuilt today.

The hotel was completed in the mid-1870s. Since its rebirth, this place has had something of a charmed life.

By the 1870s, Cape May was thriving. There were more than two thousand guest rooms in town. The Abbadon was special, though. It continued its double life. As well as its fine restaurant, it still maintained that brothel I may have told you about, as well as supporting a gambling den in the rooms off the lobby, which you apparently could only enter through a door hidden behind a bookcase.

Local authorities looked the other way at both

these activities, until one or two young local women from good families were found working in the establishment. There was a new uproar in town, led by the local paper. It looked as though the Abbadon might be closed.

And then there was the fire of 1878.

Fire prevention wasn't much of a science in the late nineteenth century. The fire brigade had horse-drawn carts that carried large barrels of water. Even with the ocean only a few blocks away, nobody had ever thought of hydrants. And all the closely packed houses were made of wood.

When the fire was over, only two hundred guest rooms remained. The Abbadon Inn, which had stood in the midst of the fire, had somehow survived, untouched by the flames.

The restaurant had a very famous cook around that time, a mulatto woman named Ebenette, who apparently was a mute. She came from New Orleans. The food was very special. Some said too special. Apparently, there were some rumors of voodoo.

But the inn was filled to capacity. The restaurant prospered. The town's attention turned away from the inn to the aftermath of the disaster. And the Abbadon thrived.

Abbadon and Lillith still seemed to own the place through the 1930s. How old was this guy, anyway? Ebenette might still have been around as well. As I said, the histories are vague. They left the place to sail for Germany, selling the property to a family named Sparks.

Even under the new ownership, the Abbadon kept up its fine history of disrepute. A speakeasy ran out of here during Prohibition, and while their brothel days were apparently over, the owners were not too particular about who rented the rooms. A new scandal would show up every year or two, or a non-scandal, like when it was discovered that Roscoe "Fatty" Arbuckle was renting a room for the summer. Somehow or other, the inn was never far from the news.

The inn passed from one generation of the Sparks family to the next. And a member of one particular generation turned out to be a bit of a gambler.

He lost it in a card game to my boss.

And now the inn belongs to Tito.

The guys rib me about my trips to the library. But what the hell, Tito seems to enjoy the stories.

He keeps changing his mind about tearing the place down. I think it all depends on whether or not he's in the mood to believe in ghosts.

For now, he'll build the luxury hotel farther down the beach. And maybe he'll bring the Abbadon back to its former glory.

I've got a feeling it'll keep on living a charmed life. I don't think the Abbadon could ever be ordinary.

But it's lost some of its spark without you.

I miss you.

Love,
Jack

She looked up from reading the letter.

"He's quite a storyteller, isn't he?" Jack said. "I can see why you wanted to read all of these."

"In the best of these letters, yes, he is." Karen looked down at the handwritten sheets before her. "Maybe it was the isolation I felt, being in a new place, the two of us not really talking, but I had the feeling that, in a way, the letters were paralleling our own situation—well, my situation, I guess, feeling lonely, then all the business with the kids playing pranks, and then the ghosts."

"So you think we have ghosts?"

How could John think they didn't? But then, he hadn't had quite the experiences she had. She looked back at her husband, trying to choose her words carefully. "There's something strange going on there. Ghosts? I don't know if they're bad or good. Maybe ghosts are neither, and that's just a value the living put on them. I almost wonder if they're trying to protect me."

How much did she want to tell him about the feeling she had had, of something cold, slipping between the sheets? She wasn't sure now how much of that had been real, how much a dream. Maybe John wasn't quite ready to hear everything yet.

"When I was falling asleep, I really felt like I sensed—something—near me. Maybe it's just the old inn, me getting used to an old, creaking building. Even if there aren't any ghosts, you can certainly see how these stories get started."

She paused, glancing back at the paper before her. "And then there was the letter that told where he hid the money."

"We could certainly use one or two more of those," John agreed.

"That's why I decided to read the rest of these. Jack Cooney spent months at the Abbadon. He'd been through all the strangeness here practically before I was even born. Maybe he can tell us something else we need to know."

There were other things she didn't add—that once or twice she had felt like Jack was speaking directly to her. Maybe that was as crazy as thinking there was a ghost between her sheets.

John smiled at her. "Well, let's see what else old Jack has to offer."

"You did what?" Angela demanded.

"He insisted," Ralph replied on the other end of the phone line. "You know the way your father is."

Angela choked back an angry response. She realized she should be more angry at herself. She should never have left Ralph to baby-sit her father. Her husband never could stand up to her old man.

"I'm here with him now," Ralph continued. "I've got him resting in his room. Whatever he thought he saw, it really took a lot out of him. I didn't think I should leave him quite yet."

"Do you think he isn't well?" She felt a moment of panic. As much as she was planning for the day Thomas would no longer be with them, Angela realized she wasn't quite ready for it yet.

"Well, he got quite upset," Ralph replied. "He's acting

a little confused. At first he wanted to get out of there, but he keeps talking about wanting to go back. He saw something there."

"Something?" she prompted.

"He won't tell me any more about it."

"Did *you* see anything?"

Ralph paused before he answered. "Don't laugh at me."

That surprised Angela again. She agreed that she wouldn't.

"I saw things that I can't explain. After being in that place, I think I might believe in ghosts."

Ghosts? Ralph was the most levelheaded person she had ever known. Angela didn't know what to say.

"We never saw John and Karen," Ralph said. "I doubt they ever knew we were there."

"And he wants to go back there."

"He insists on going back there. Although I think I've convinced him to wait until morning."

"Let me come over and take a look at him."

She hung up the phone.

If her father was unwell, they should probably get him back to Manhattan and his doctors as quickly as possible. Maybe they could push up tomorrow's meeting to first thing in the morning, then drive him back to New York by afternoon.

There might be a positive side to this as well. Perhaps there was some way to avoid an angry scene between father and son at the Abbadon. She didn't care what that took. Maybe the ghosts could scare some sense into the old man.

* * *

Karen pulled the next letter from the pile and began to read it aloud.

Dear Lucy,

Tito's gone off the deep end.

He's seeing them all the time now—the ghosts, I mean. Whenever he's alone, day or night, they seem to come for him. And I think he's convinced some of the others. They've started seeing things, too. I'm beginning to think I'm the only one here who hasn't gone crazy.

It doesn't help that two of our people are missing. In fact, I think it was those disappearances that started all of this. Some rival organization is out to get us. Tito has stepped on too many toes. But I can't get people to see that it's real people, and not ghosts, that have got our number.

But whoever it is, they're good. They don't leave a trace. Still, some of our guys are just plain gone. And everybody's on edge. Then they found Uncle Freddy dead, with that knife in his chest— would ghosts use knives? And Sal the Barber got strangled just outside the inn. It was looking more like we had real enemies, the kind you can actually kill with a gun. Seeing those two guys dead actually helped the rest of the gang—I guessed it focused us, let us get a little bit away from our fears.

Not that that lasted for long.

It didn't really get bad until we found Vinnie Fishhooks upstairs, with that look on his face.

And not a single mark on his body. That sent Tito right over the edge.

He talks about the ghosts now like they were his old friends. He thinks the ghosts were always here. Dormant, beneath the surface, waiting to come out. They just needed the right stuff to wake them up. What's the right stuff? I think I told you before, books I read said ghosts are drawn to life, to large groups, maybe to activity, maybe to emotion, maybe to violence.

Well, there's been plenty of activity, lots of emotion, and way too much violence around here. See? Tito's even got me explaining the ghosts!

But why here? Tito's convinced that something is different about the Abbadon, something maybe brought by the original owners or their voodoo cook, something that gave this inn its charmed life. But he says there was a price to pay.

"Maybe everyone who has ever died within these walls stays as a ghost," Tito says. "They make us see things, things that aren't true, but that we want to see. I don't know if they kill us, or we kill ourselves."

When your boss starts talking like that, it's no wonder everyone is a little gone. When your boss believes stuff like this, everybody starts jumping at shadows, pulling out guns at the slightest noise, losing whatever common sense any of us have ever had.

It's a good way to get all of us killed, no matter

*who or what is after us. And I can see no way to
stop it.*

Maybe I'll end up seeing ghosts, too.

*Pray for me,
Jack.*

Karen looked up at John.

"Well, that's pretty direct. Somebody here believed
in ghosts."

"I think I agree with Jack. It sounds pretty crazy to me."

The phone rang. John picked it up. The conversation
was short and surprising. He slammed the phone back
in place, then took a deep breath.

"That was my sister. My father dragged Ralph into
the Abbadon this afternoon."

"Without talking to either of us?" Karen thought
back through her day. "Oh, dear. I was probably taking
a nap."

"How could you have known? My father wants to go
back there, first thing tomorrow morning. I agreed to
meet them. I want to get this over with."

He looked at Karen.

"Your pal Jack's batting a thousand." John shook his
head. "Or maybe it was his boss, Tito."

"What do you mean?"

"Apparently, my father saw a ghost."

NINETEEN

Janet Frost hadn't slept at all. Her husband was gone.

Don hadn't come home last night. When she had first returned from the prayer meeting with her son in tow, she had thought she had seen him on the side of the house next to the Abbadon. He had been talking to a woman, who looked a little like Phyllis, when she was younger. Janet didn't think Phyllis had a sister.

Janet had called his name. He hadn't replied. That wasn't like Don. When she came into the house she discovered he had left a bottle of vodka out in the open. That wasn't like Don, either. It felt like he had ignored all the talks they had had over these past months and was ready to throw away his marriage, like he didn't care a thing for his current life. And that worried her more than anything.

She had heard of middle-aged men just disappearing, going to start a new life someplace else. Was that what

Don was going to do? Maybe she had been too hard on him. Maybe she had spent too much time finding herself and not enough looking out for her family. Maybe there could have been some way to have kept Kenny out of J.J.'s life. And maybe there was some way she could have found to listen to her husband.

Not that she had given up on him yet. She had gone looking for him, all around the neighborhood. She had even tried the basement door of the place next door, though after his last experience down there, she doubted he would go there again.

The door had been locked, anyway. There were no lights in the Abbadon's windows. The hotel was totally still.

She had walked one more time around her house. Her husband's car was still in the driveway. She hadn't heard anybody else driving away. If he left with that woman, he must have walked. It made as much sense as anything.

Toward morning, J.J. had gotten up and come down to the kitchen. He said he had had a dream about his dad, that his father was visiting Kenny now. It just showed how upset J.J. still was over the loss of his friend. How much worse would it be if J.J.'s father ran off as well?

Why would Don leave without a word?

She remembered the other reason they hadn't bought the inn next door. It was the way her mother talked about the place. Like there was something unclean about it, something corrupt, something from the old days that would never go away.

And then there had been that murder, when Janet was a girl. That made the place doubly evil.

Janet's mother had been a superstitious woman. Her

daughter had always discounted nine-tenths of what the old woman said. But Janet had listened to her about the Abbadon.

Why?

Just for her own peace of mind, Janet decided she would go over and talk to the new owners of the Abbadon the next time she saw them.

He had seen Emily. How could he tell them?

Thomas Dalton could barely understand it himself. Emily was dead. He knew Emily was dead.

But John had always been Emily's favorite.

He had no idea how ghosts worked. Before yesterday afternoon, he hadn't even believed in them. Emily had died in Connecticut. What would bring her spirit here? Maybe John's connection with his mother had brought a piece of her with him, a piece that had manifested itself on the third floor of the Abbadon Inn.

It had been a shock. It would have been for anyone. He had been overwhelmed at first. He had needed time to sort things out, a few minutes peace without Angela and Ralph acting like mother hens at his bedside.

They had left him after a couple hours, after he had eaten a room-service sandwich and assured them both he was quite all right. Ralph had talked about seeing a ghost. Thomas had agreed, as calmly as he could, that he had seen something. He was careful not to mention Emily's name.

He needed to go back there as soon as possible.

Ralph had seen her, too, he knew that. But Ralph didn't know Emily the way he did, had only met her a few times at the end of her life when Emily no longer had the energy or the beauty of her youth. But her ghost had all of that, all of that and so much more.

And she wanted Thomas. He could tell that from the first time he looked at her.

He was exhausted, but he had had trouble sleeping. He had fallen asleep sometime after midnight, and he had woken up sometime before dawn. He had opened the curtains in his room. The world outside was a uniform gray. He doubted it would get much brighter. It looked like there might be a storm coming.

It didn't matter. He had to get back there and find Emily. He had convinced his daughter to reschedule their meeting with his son for nine this morning. Almost four hours from now.

He would take them all up to the third floor. He wanted them all to see her. Angela and John and their spouses. It was too bad he hadn't gotten his eldest son to come down here as well.

Emily would listen. Emily would understand.

Four hours.

It seemed like it would be an eternity.

Karen looked over the letters again as they ate breakfast in their kitchenette.

The last few were not much help. They were all short, like those odd, earlier notes Jack had written.

Dear Lucy,

  I know that somebody is out to get us, but they haven't gotten to me yet. I'm careful.

*The others haven't been so lucky. We found
Gino dead in the basement yesterday, and now
Tito's girlfriend has disappeared, too. Some of
the guys want to believe that she had just had
enough and left on her own, but Tito thinks different. He's ready to run himself.*

I'll write again when I can.

J.

Most of the later letters were only two or three lines
like that, with thoughts like *If I don't get out now, I
don't think I ever will* and *I think this is the final time I
can write you.*

She showed them to John.

"Cheerful stuff," was his only comment.

"I think he was losing it," Karen replied. "Whatever
was going on was really getting to him."

"It's almost like you feel sorry for this guy."

He was right. She had invested a lot in these letters.
"Well, he was one of the first friends I made at the
Abbadon."

And unlike Eddie—she thought but didn't say aloud—
a real flesh-and-blood man who might return her lonely
advances, she could feel as much as she wanted about a
person who only existed on the page.

She had put a couple of boxes of clothing together to
take over, the beginning of the move to their new per-
manent home, their business, their hope for the future.

She shook her head. Far too much was riding on this
meeting with John's father.

She thought about what Jack had said about the

ghosts, about how they were looking for the stuff of the living, human drama, human emotion.

In the next few hours, she bet the ghosts would see plenty of anger and tons of family drama. She hoped the spirits appreciated what the living Daltons were doing for them.

"I think I'm ready to go," she said to John.

She decided to take the box of letters with her and put them back in the kitchen, where they belonged.

Eddie didn't know what to do with himself.

It was Friday. He'd taken a day off. A day he wouldn't see Karen Dalton. Stan was off with his wife, planning some home-improvement projects of their own. Eddie sensed a kid in their future.

And there wasn't anything more to do around Eddie's house. He had gone kind of crazy in the months after his wife had left, replacing the old bathroom, putting in new kitchen appliances, completely redoing his workroom—anything to keep busy. Plus, he guessed, he wanted to get rid of everything that reminded him of his wife. And, as an extra benefit, working all the time also meant he didn't have time to meet anybody new, or even acknowledge his feelings.

Until he met Karen.

He hadn't realized how dissatisfied he had been with his life until she had shown up.

It was starting to snow outside. It looked like winter wasn't done with them yet.

Eddie threw on his jacket and gloves. He didn't want

the weather to box him in. He would just get in his truck and go.

He decided he'd take a drive back into town. He would just do some of his errands for next week a little early.

That meant he would drive by the inn. He wouldn't stop. He wouldn't hope for a glimpse of Karen. He didn't want to be a stalker or something.

His feelings for Karen had woken him up. Now he had to move on. Who knew? Maybe, on his errands, he could run into somebody new?

Angela had never seen her father so agitated.

"I will not delay our meeting. You've been trying to keep me out of that hotel since we first heard of John's interest in the place!"

"I hear there's quite a storm coming through. I don't know if we want to be out driving in it." She was actually more worried about her father walking around in it—the weather forecasts had predicted a lot of ice.

The weather also meant they couldn't drive back to Manhattan. She wanted to be able to get help if her father started acting strangely. It did no good to panic. Even if she couldn't get him to his private doctors, Cape May was a pretty civilized resort town. There must be plenty of good hospitals in southern New Jersey.

Her father would not sit still. He kept getting up from his chair to pace around.

"I need all of you there with me. There's something in that hotel. I want us to find it together!"

"We'll go." She looked out the window. Only a few

innocent snowflakes were falling so far, no indication of the fury of the storm to come.

She waved her husband over to the far side of the room. Her father glared moodily at the TV.

"Ralph," she said in hushed tones, "I don't know about this. Is my father—" She wanted to say "losing it" but that sounded too harsh. "—doing all right here?"

Ralph looked to where the old man sat down on the bed, only to push himself back off it a moment later.

"He does seem agitated, even for your father."

Angela smiled a bit at that. Even at the best of times, Thomas Dalton did not have a reputation for being calm.

"I have no idea what we saw," Ralph continued. "I don't know if we saw anything at all. But something strange happened there. It wasn't entirely his imagination."

Angela found this all very frustrating. "But if you're not sure what you saw, who's to say it will happen again? Will that make him even more agitated?"

"Anything that happens will tell us something—maybe it will tell us more about your father's condition than anything about that old inn."

Unfortunately, Angela thought, her husband was probably right.

"I'll get the car started and bring it around front." Ralph called out to the old man. "Fifteen minutes, Dad!"

"About time!" his father-in-law called back.

One way or another, Angela supposed her father was right about that, too.

TWENTY

Karen, John, and the Abbadon Inn were ready.

Karen didn't like the waiting. Angela and the others were late, delayed no doubt by the growing storm. The few lone snowflakes they had seen on their way over here had been pretty, but the wind was beginning to pick up, and she could hear it howl through the loose boards and bang against the windows of the inn. She guessed it was going to be a dramatic day all around.

John waited in the lobby, not saying much of anything, steeling himself, she guessed, for what was to come. There were so many ways old Thomas could attack you, she didn't know how he could possibly plan for anything and everything.

Maybe Thomas would surprise them and not attack

at all. Maybe the ghosts would all come out and introduce themselves. Maybe pigs would fly.

She went back to the kitchen to return the box to its
cupboard—where it belonged—the place of honor she
had given it, she supposed. It was a part of the inn, it felt
right here.

She saw a flash of yellow as she opened the cupboard
door. What was this?

It was another piece of paper; a note that had slipped
away from the others.

My darling:

   *No matter, what happens, I will protect you. We
will be together at last.*

   J.

Jack and Lucy, Lucy and Jack. Even though he never
talked about why she had left, she knew he loved her so
dearly. It would be a shame if they had never gotten
back together.

Eddie had pointed out that the letters were here. So
she must have come back to him at some point.

She wondered if any of the neighbors might know
what happened to them. Or if she, like Jack, might go
and look it up in the local library.

She stuffed the final note in the pocket of her sweater
and walked toward the front of the inn.

The banging on the front door was loud enough to be
heard even over the wailing wind. She rushed through
the dining room to join her husband.

* * *

John met his father at the door. Ralph and Angela stood behind him. Angela started to say something, but their father pushed his way into the house before anyone else could start a conversation.

"We meet at last," his father spoke abruptly, looking around the lobby rather than at his son. "You're a very difficult person to track down."

John sighed. He would never expect his father to be polite.

"I never asked you to come here," he replied evenly. "It would have been easier to leave well enough alone."

The old man laughed dismissively. "You know I don't work that way. You are my son, and you will be my son until the day I die."

John knew what that was code for. "Which means you make the rules."

"I never told you otherwise. This is not a democracy."

He wasn't going to be drawn into one of his father's tirades. "This house has nothing to do with you."

"This house is mine!" his father shot back. The old man was staring at him now. "Everything you own is mine!"

"Why can't you leave any of us alone!" John realized they were screaming at each other already.

"You know why. I'm the one who gave you everything—all of you. Because I have jurisdiction over everything. I'm the boss, pure and simple. You can take something from me, but I'll always get it back. Emily understands." He looked across the room. "Don't you, Emily?"

Now the old man was calling out to his mother? Did

he expect an answer from a woman who was two years dead? John always thought his father was crazy, but this was the first time he could really see it.

The storm rattled the windows.

Ralph looked around the room. "I don't think we should be here."

"That's the problem with all of you!" Thomas shot back. "No guts!" He hit the nearest wall with the back of his hand. "This is mine. It was paid for with my money! Money that Emily stole from me!"

Even Angela couldn't take that. "Dad. There was a court settlement."

"Courts! What do they know about real ownership? What do they know about who deserves to own it all?"

He swung back to glare at John. "You're hiding her from me. But I'm too smart for that. I found her, and I will have her again!"

A great, groaning noise came from somewhere inside the inn, as though the whole structure was shifting under the force of the weather.

Thomas spun to look at Ralph.

"Where?" he demanded.

"Upstairs," Ralph replied. "But I don't think—"

"You never think! Without me, none of you would ever act! I'm going back up there! And any of you who want to know the truth should follow me!"

Angela tried to restrain him, but Thomas shook her hand away. He walked rapidly toward the stairs.

Karen was halfway through the dining room when she heard the whole house groan. The lights flickered. She had heard raised voices in the other room, but the storm was so loud outside that she couldn't make out the words.

She hurried to join the others. The lights flickered off for good. She stopped. They had candles back in the kitchen. Should she feel her way back there or try to forge ahead and join the others? It was still morning, and as dark as the storm was, a bit of light filtered into the room. She blinked, letting her eyes adjust. She thought she heard someone moving out in the hallway.

"Is someone there?" she asked.

"Lucy?" a man's voice replied.

Ralph knew this would not be good.

As bad as he had felt in this place before, now it was far worse. It seemed as if the power of the storm had awakened something. Before, he could sense eyes behind the wall. Now, he could see them staring out of the wallpaper, waiting for the proper moment to strike.

They all needed to get out of here. But the old man was already heading up the stairs. His wife and his brother-in-law both followed.

"Angela, no!" he called. But she didn't even look back. The three disappeared around the corner of the stairs, on their way to the second floor.

He could let Thomas go. He might even be able to ignore John. But he had to save Angela.

Ralph hurried up the steps after them.

Eddie pulled over to the side of the road when he saw the car out front and the Abbadon's door wide open. In the middle of a storm? It looked like something was wrong.

He got out of his truck as Janet Frost walked over from the house next door, and together they approached the inn.

He pointed at the door in front of them. "It was wide open. I think the wind blew it open. I don't know if anybody else is here."

Janet shook her head. "I saw them all going in earlier. They have visitors."

Maybe everything was all right then, Eddie thought. Maybe he should just be a good neighbor, close the door, and be on his way.

"Come inside for a minute!" Janet insisted. Eddie supposed a minute couldn't hurt. Janet closed the door behind them. "I'm looking for my Don."

"Your husband?" Eddie asked. "Do you think he's here?"

Janet nodded her head. "I think everybody's in here. I should have realized it before." She walked into the lobby. Eddie followed.

"My mother used to talk of ghosts," Janet continued. "I always pooh-poohed her. But maybe she made me believe a little bit in them, too."

She shook her head. "Such terrible things that happened here. Like that gangster that killed his girlfriend."

He only knew the name of one gangster who'd lived in the Abbadon.

"Jack Cooney?" Eddie asked.

"You remember, too? He buried her in the yard. Lucy Searles. She came from Wildwood. She disappeared in sixty-one. Her body got washed up by the big storm back in sixty-two. He disappeared, too, in the storm. They never found his body."

"Wait a minute! Jack killed Lucy?"

Janet nodded her head. "They think he strangled her two weeks after he got here. Afterward, he used to go around everywhere, asking folks if they'd seen her. She was buried outside for the better part of a year."

All those letters Karen had found had been written to a dead woman. That's why the letters were here. Jack Cooney had had nowhere else to send them.

Karen wasn't going to like that news one bit. But where was Karen?

"This place has a colorful history," Janet said. "But I think the color is mostly blood-red." She looked around the room. "I've got to find Don. I was thinking I'd start in the basement."

They heard an enormous crash from above.

"Or maybe not," Janet added.

"It sounds like the storm wants to tear this place apart," Eddie said.

Eddie heard a woman scream from somewhere deeper inside the inn.

"Who's there?" Eddie called. "Do you need help?"

"Let's go see," Janet said, leading the way toward the back of the inn. "I have a feeling Don's back there, too. If he's anywhere at all."

Ralph caught up with the others where they had stopped on the third floor.

"Where is she?" Thomas was screaming at his son. "Where are you hiding her?"

"What are you talking about?" John shouted back.

The old man started pushing at his son with the heels

of his hands. John stumbled back in surprise while his father screamed, "I will not be denied! I will not be denied! I will not be denied!"

John slapped his father across the face. "Stop it! You're not making any sense!"

His father staggered back, glaring at his son. In all the years he had worked for him, Ralph didn't think he had ever seen such hatred in the old man's eyes.

The gale hit the house with renewed force.

A window exploded inward with the force of the wind, bits of glass flying everywhere. The room was filled with swirling snow.

Angela looked scared. "What's going on here? Can the wind do something like that?"

His wife was right to be scared, Ralph thought. "I think it's more than just the wind," he replied. But he could see them now, seeping out of the wall to dance through the spiraling snow.

He had thought he'd be safer with others here. He was sure a group of people would discourage the spirits. But he had no idea there would be this many; that the ghosts would outnumber them ten to one. Maybe they were emboldened by the storm, or by so many people coming to a place that had been empty for so long. He couldn't know.

Still they came, spreading out from the walls like an ever-widening stain. He thought there were a hundred of them. And they were looking for what?

Whatever allowed Ralph to see them also let him know that they wanted something added to their never-ending existence. That they wanted to make the living suffer. But more than anything, they wanted company. Company that would stay with them forever.

He grabbed Angela's arm. "Can you see them?"

"See who?" Angela asked. "The room is full of snow!"

"Stay close beside me!" he called. "It's not safe here!"

"Emily!" the old man shouted. He rushed into the gale.

Angela gasped. "What are they?" she whispered. The snow around them was taking human shape, so even she could see them now.

The cold white shapes moved toward the living. And still they came. The room was filling with the snow-covered dead.

John tried to stay close to the others, but it felt as if the wind was trying to push them apart. Their father had vanished, and Ralph was halfway across the room. The inn seemed caught in the middle of the storm. Or worse. Shapes moved through the snow behind the half-built walls.

"I have to find Karen!" John called to his sister. He had thought she would follow them up here. Then all hell broke loose. What if she was in danger downstairs?

"But what about Dad?"

Ralph looked into the maelstrom surrounding him. "I'll find him." He nodded to John. "You take Angela downstairs!"

"Do you think it's any safer down there?" Angela called over the howling wind.

"It can't be any worse!" Ralph shouted back.

"Be safe!" Angela said as her brother led her toward the stairs. "Come down to us soon!"

Ralph grinned at her. "Hey. I always do my best."

* * *

Thomas was stumbling through the dark alone. He had been surrounded by snow one minute, following Emily's voice. He must have stepped through a doorway and gotten out of the cold. The snow and the wind were gone. But he could barely see. The room was as dark as midnight.

"Hello?" he called.

Where was he? Why couldn't he hear the others?

"Dad?"

He knew that voice. His oldest son, his namesake.

"Dad, are you here?"

Thomas had intended to call him to come down. But never did, had he? Thomas frowned. He must have. His son stepped out of the darkness.

"Tip! I'm so glad you're here."

His son grinned. Thomas had rarely seen a smile so wide. "Well, what could I do, when you wanted the whole family together."

So Tip hadn't betrayed him like the rest of his family. Thomas felt a great fondness for his oldest son. "You know, Tip, we hardly talk at all."

"That will change, Father. I'm sure it will. See who else is here?"

A vision of beauty stepped out of nowhere. "Thomas. It's been so long."

Thomas' heart almost stopped beating. "Emily!"

She held out her ivory arms. "Come here, Thomas. I've missed you so. We can be together forever."

"Forever?" Thomas shook his head. "I'm sorry,

Emily. My heart's weak. My life's almost done. We don't have that long."

Tip laughed at that. "I told you he was sharp! Old man! We don't have long at all!"

Thomas frowned. Tip and Emily were changing. Shifting into something not quite human. Something with a lot of teeth.

"We're going to teach you a lesson, Thomas," the thing that had been Emily hissed. "A family lesson."

A dozen more like them stepped out of the darkness.

"We're going to teach you to share."

Thomas screamed and tried to back away, but they were behind him, too. They had more than teeth. Their hands were like claws, digging out great gouts of his flesh.

"Oh, Thomas!" he heard through the pain. "We can just eat you all up."

Ralph knew the ghosts were all beyond that door.

The storm had changed again. Sometimes it looked like a score of figures, sometimes it only looked like snow. The wind seemed to have died down a bit, the worst of its fury spent.

Ralph wondered if the inn had gotten what it wanted.

He took a deep breath and stepped through the door. A hundred frost-white shapes were crawling over each other, on the floor. Underneath them all, Ralph somehow knew, was something living—barely living.

The snow shifted. The building moaned.

But now it lived no more.

The things stepped back, away from what had drawn their attention. Ralph looked at the bare spot at the center of the floor.

His father-in-law had been in here once. Now there was only a brown stain on the floor.

The shapes turned to regard him.

"No!" Ralph cried. "I will not allow this! Get out of here! Get out!"

With a silent scream, the shapes rushed toward him as one.

Karen didn't seem able to move. The figure in the shadows looked like a man. But Karen didn't think it was even human.

"We'll be together, always," it said softly.

"Jack?" Karen asked. "Jack Cooney?"

"I knew you'd remember, Lucy." The shape took a step toward her. Its features grew no clearer. It was as though it brought the shadows wherever it traveled. "I knew you'd come back. That's why I couldn't leave. If I only waited long enough . . ."

"Long enough?" If this person, or thing, was Jack, it had been impossibly long. "It's been twenty-five years!"

"You're joking, Lucy. You've always had a problem being serious. I never liked that about you." The shape was growing closer. "We've hardly been apart at all. The only time that matters is the time that we're together."

"You don't understand!" Karen said, hoarsely. *"I'm not Lucy!"*

The figure hesitated. It's image seemed to fade for

an instant before it returned. "You're not Lucy? But I wrote the note just for you. I wrote all the notes for you. We were meant to be together, no matter what." It reached a hand out toward her. "I'll protect you from all the others."

Karen looked down at the fingers that were almost touching her. The rest of the thing was dark, but its hand was bone-white.

"I'm not Lucy!" Karen was almost crying.

"You're not Lucy?" The thing in the shadows hesitated, fading again for an instant. Karen stared as the shape reformed, looking more like a man than ever before. The fabric of his suit coat rustled as he moved his arm. She could see small points of reflected light at the place his eyes should be.

"Of course not," Jack Cooney said, almost wistfully. "I remember now. I killed Lucy."

He grabbed for her arm.

"But you'll do."

"There!" Janet called as they stepped into the dining room.

Eddie could see Karen standing in the dim light, looking very scared. And, somewhere near her, he thought he saw the outline of a man.

"Karen!" he called. "Over here!"

She didn't move. Was she that scared?

Well, if she wouldn't come to them, he would go to her. Eddie moved quickly toward the shape. The darkness shimmered, as though it was turning toward him. Eddie lunged forward with a shout, ready to tackle whatever it was and move it away from Karen.

His body flew through the shape as though there were nothing there. Eddie cried out as he hit the wall, hard. A searing pain shot up his leg.

The thing that was Jack Cooney looked back at her. It waved to the others who had entered the room.

"None of these people mean anything to you. Not like you mean to me. Come now, and we'll be together always."

Karen wanted to run, but her legs still would not move. She could feel herself drifting toward the shadow, almost as if she was floating. The man-shape spread his arms before her, ready to embrace her, to draw her in forever.

"Come to me, and you will be my Lucy, and we will be complete."

She felt her eyes begin to close as the shadow rose above her. She felt the strength drain from her as the cold fingers reached to touch her shoulders and bleed away any warmth she had ever known.

The shadow leaned forward to kiss her.

"Karen!"

Her eyes flew open. Her husband was here. Her life was here.

"John!" The sound tore from deep within her heart, out past the chill air in her throat, the blue tinge growing on her lips.

The shadow seemed to waver. "Come now," it said, softly.

She turned her head away from the thing that was once Jack Cooney. She saw her husband John running toward her across the room, until her view was blocked by shadow.

"Lucy! We must be together."

Karen shook her head. The voice was everywhere, as though it wanted to overwhelm her, to cover her entirely in darkness.

"Lucy and Jack. The way it was meant to be. I made a mistake. I can make it up to you. It will be different, You'll see."

Different? Karen was finding it hard to concentrate. What did she want?

What did Lucy want?

"Karen!"

John left his sister in the doorway to rush into the dining room. Karen seemed to be fading into shadow. He ran ahead, but lost sight of his wife in the gloom. He stopped short of a wall. He felt as if the whole room was shifting around him.

"John!" someone called to him.

He turned to see Eddie on the floor. His leg was twisted in an unnatural angle. John knelt down to see if he could help, but Eddie waved him away.

"It's Jack Cooney," Eddie managed, pain seeping through his words. "That's who's after Karen."

"Jack? The guy who wrote the letters?"

"Yeah. Except Jack killed the woman he wrote the letters to. And he wants Karen now."

John looked up. He saw his wife's frightened face flash among the shadows.

"Karen! I'm coming for you!"

Karen heard her name. Her husband's cries brought her back to life.

"Lucy," Jack whispered.

No. She would not lose herself again.

"There is no Lucy!" she screamed. "You killed her!"

"There will always be a Lucy. I recognized you when you first read my letters. You know you can be my Lucy. You'll see."

"Karen!" Her husband's voice cut through the haze surrounding her, the word loud and clear and close.

"Lucy!" the shadow's voice was even nearer. "I need to hear your voice. Say my name. Lucy and Jack. Lucy and—"

"No!" John's living voice shouted. "Karen. She's Karen. My wife."

Her husband was suddenly there beside her. He touched Karen's arm, and she was filled with warmth. How had she become so cold?

"Lucy is dead!" her husband called out to the room. "Jack is dead!"

"Don't listen!" The shadow's voice, still insistent, seemed to be fading away. "The ghosts are all around us. They've got what they came for!" The figure seemed to solidify for one final instant, so that it almost looked like a man. "Lucy! I can save you from all of them. I can save you forever!"

"Save me from what?" Karen had found her voice again. "Lucy has been dead for twenty-five years!"

"Not that long!" the voice cried, faintly "Never that long!"

John wrapped his arms around her. "You're safe now, Karen. We'll get away from this place forever."

She wrapped her arms around her husband as well.

"I'm so glad I found you," John said.

"Not half so glad as me." Karen looked at the fading shadow still reaching toward her. "They're both dead? Lucy and Jack?"

"Jack killed Lucy," her husband said, and Karen felt the cold once again brush her skin.

"Yes. He told me that," she said, clinging to her husband.

Lucy. The word was barely a whisper on the wind.

"Get away from me," she said. "You're just another ghost!"

The wind howled one final time, a sound of anger, and grief, and loss. And then the room was still.

The shadow was gone. The lights flickered back on.

"Ghosts," Janet said. "You just have to know how to handle them." She sighed. "My Donny was here. He asked me to dance. I turned him down." She made a sour face. "He was always a terrible dancer."

"Are they gone?" John asked.

"Who knows?" Janet shook her head. "If they are, then Don's gone with them."

John took Karen in his arms as Janet went to tend to Eddie. John and Karen held each other for a very long time.

TWENTY-ONE

It was over, but it would never be over.

John stood outside the Abbadon, watching the movers take the never-unpacked boxes away. After what had happened, they decided they would never run the inn themselves.

Their father had vanished in the storm. They would have some trouble clearing up the estate, but Angela now controlled all the money. And their father had never changed his will. The money would go to the three children equally.

They had kept Eddie and Stan on to do the basic repairs to the hotel, even though Eddie was moving a little slow with his broken leg. Eddie had been a little dubious about coming back for the first day or two, but had finally relented when Stan had started back to work without him. Whatever had come to the Abbadon during that storm had not returned.

When the storm was over, they had found Ralph on the third floor in a state of shock. With two weeks now past, he had begun to make some simple sounds. There appeared to be nothing physically wrong with him. The doctors were hopeful he would recover. And, as Angela said, "I'm going to make sure to take care of him. He certainly took care of me."

Afterward, Karen had pulled the final note from Jack Cooney from her pocket. Or what she said was the final note. All she had found was a blank piece of paper.

Janet Frost had barely spoken to them since that day. She'd told Eddie that she didn't blame them, she blamed the inn. And herself, a little. She sent J.J. away to his aunt and uncle in Ohio, at least for a while, and tried to go back to business as usual. But she said that she thought her B-and-B might have a ghost of its own now.

As for John and Karen, working with Angela, they now had the money to buy and develop a dozen properties down the shore. Which they would probably do. But not in Cape May, not anywhere even remotely close to the Abbadon Inn, which was, once more, listed for sale with Cape Realty.